Fred Miller

The Training of a Craftsman

Fred Miller

The Training of a Craftsman

ISBN/EAN: 9783337366377

Printed in Europe, USA, Canada, Australia, Japan

Cover: Foto ©Andreas Hilbeck / pixelio.de

More available books at **www.hansebooks.com**

" Here, work enough to watch
The master work, and catch
Hints of the proper craft, tricks of the tool's true play."
RABBI BEN EZRA.

THE TRAINING
OF A CRAFTSMAN
WRITTEN BY FRED MILLER
ILLUSTRATED BY MANY
WORKERS IN THE ART CRAFTS

TRUSLOVE & COMBA,
NEW YORK. 1898.

"The noblest thing that is said now, or shall be said hereafter, is, that what is profitable is honourable and what is hurtful is base."

PLATO.

"And only the master shall praise us, and only the master shall blame,
And no one shall work for money, and no one shall work for fame,
But each for the joy of the working, and each, in his separate star,
Shall draw the Thing as he sees It for the God of Things as They are!"

RUDYARD KIPLING.

"Wherefore I perceive that there is nothing better, than that a man should rejoice in his own works; for that is his portion."

ECCLESIASTES.

TO THE READER.

— ◆

THE following little book is the outcome of a series of articles I contributed to THE ART JOURNAL on "Art Crafts and Craftsmen." My object then was to bring to the notice of the reader, through the medium of illustrations, the work of some few representative craftsmen, with a few personal notes, the result of conversations with the craftsmen themselves, and also a general survey of the work being done to-day in some of the leading crafts.

In the pages of THE ART JOURNAL for the last five years were many illustrations bearing upon the subject, and I have made a selection of these to add to the others, because illustrations in a work like this are its most valuable features, and as these, with the exception of the Nature Notes in the first chapter, are taken from the work of some of our leading craftsmen, this book should, *on that ground*, have a value, as the student can see at a glance the trend of present-day craftsmanship and be stimulated and helped thereby.

With a few unavoidable exceptions only modern work is illustrated, as that wrought by our contemporaries has an interest for us which old work, however excellent, cannot have, not being the outcome of the Time spirit (*Zeitgeist*).

Now that it is realised that the craftsman can be an artist whether carving a pew-end or beating a finger-plate just as much as if he were engaged in painting a picture, the work of to-day is more virile, vehement, and veracious than it has been any time within this century, and to detach it, therefore, from all other work seemed to me the best way to give the present book value and distinction.

Though I address myself mainly to the student, I venture to hope that this work may find its way into the hands of some few patrons, for nothing is so crushing to the earnest craftsman as to find that, though he stand in the market-place waiting to be hired, no one comes by him to engage his services, and he is forced in consequence to remain dumb because no one will enable him to give his ego utterance. As much responsibility rests with the patron as the craftsman in the production of good work, and to see that which is not of good report preferred is a serious hindrance to progress in the art crafts. It needs nearly as much training to be an intelligent appreciator as it does to be a producer, though to be as accomplished as the latter requires a very real and long apprenticeship.

To the patron I say, Search out for yourself a craftsman to do the particular work you require, and having found him trust him, and ask him to give you of his best; and to the craftsman I say, Before all else be faithful to the best traditions of your craft, and put yourself thoroughly into all you do.

FRED MILLER.

CONTENTS.

LIST OF ARTISTS

WHOSE DESIGNS ARE REPRODUCED IN THIS BOOK.

The numbers given are those under the Illustrations.

———◆———

THE TRAINING OF A CRAFTSMAN.

•

CHAPTER I.

THE CRAFTSMAN AND NATURE.

THE idea that designing can be taught as a youth can be turned out a carpenter after so many years' apprenticeship is one of those fallacies which die hard. Designing is a purely mental process, and may be defined as imagination playing over and arranging forms and lines into pleasing combinations, and is, in all essentials, the same quality that gives us musicians, and painters, and poets, and the last we know are born, not made.

It may be said too, in passing, that Rhythm in music and poetry is what distribution and balance are in design, but such an inquiry would take us outside our immediate subject, which is "The Training of a Craftsman."

Design cannot be taught, though much may be learned from the study of the methods of those who have worked before us. A teacher may therefore perform some service by bringing before the student's attention that which he

considers of good report—a method Ruskin followed at
Oxford. The drawback to this is that the student very

Fig. 1.

possibly does not see the merit in the particular example
you put before him. Your critical faculty is sharper than
his, and it may be some years before the student is capable

of appreciating what begets your approbation. Looking back to student days, I must admit that I was incapable of seeing the merit in a good many works which were put before me as examples worthy my respect and veneration, and which I have only slowly learned to appreciate. They

Fig. 2.

were dumb for many years, though now they speak. In one's art education one begins by indiscriminately admiring the rococo, the flamboyant, the bizarre. The mesh of one's mind in time adjusts itself until it throws away the chaff and retains the grain, and the best art training is the one that enables the student the more quickly to reach this

mental state. It is certain that no student can afford to
ignore the work of other days and peoples, not for imitation,
but to widen his sympathies and to cultivate the critical
faculty. which as a student he is probably wholly without.
The reason why you reject one class of work and accept
another can only come with time. In youth one admires
fervently and hates blindly. One was such a bundle of
prejudices too in those days, for when one is young one
cannot see the good in everything ; such catholicity is only
reached after much mental warfare and the breaking down
of many prejudices. Youth is vehement and antagonistic
because it is wildly enthusiastic. It should be so. The
fever will get out of your blood quite quickly enough : love
and hate strongly until you can do so with judgment and
without bias.

I am inclined to think that old work has hitherto been
thrust too prominently before the student to the exclusion
of all else. with the result that he wearies of it, and would
consign it to its fitting burial place, the gloomy recesses of
a museum. The same old casts which for years have hung
up in schools of art have bred contempt because of one's
familiarity with them. The work that is being wrought by
our contemporaries is, as it should be, of a more stimulating
and vivid interest to a student than any efforts of a bygone
age, and I have therefore excluded old examples in this
work, save in a few instances, so that the reader may
learn. if he will, of h's contemporaries by seeing what
they are doing.

But whether the student study old work or modern he
must remember that nature is, after all, the fountain head of
inspiration and the source of all strength ; all other teaching

and training should be considered at best as second-hand knowledge. Just as reading should not take the place of

Fig. 3.

observation, so craftsmen's work should be considered as a commentary on Nature ; and whatever else an art teacher may do for the student he should always lead him back to nature, though he may assist him by showing the student how other craftsmen have utilised the suggestions and hints received from nature. Nature is the raw material wherewith you garment your *ego*, and "old clothes," though

NUSTURTIUM

Fig. 4.

they may serve as guides, are not what you should dress yourself in. The world is wanting to see what freshness of invention, what new combinations you are waiting to give it. It requires your personality to be stamped vehemently on all you do.

Every student has to ask himself " How am I going to gain the necessary knowledge. and how use it when it is gained ? " I can here only speak from my own experience. and that I place at the service of my readers.

It is now more than twelve years since I wrote four of the handbooks in Wyman's technical series,* which were in the main illustrated by me, and those twelve years have changed my point of view a good deal, and I hope widened my sympathies. Looking back I can see, I think. in what

Fig. 5.

I was deficient in those days, for when I was a pupil, over twenty years ago, the art crafts were denied the position now given them. The individual was lost sight of in the " firm," and as I was a " hand " in a firm of glass painters I merely acquired a certain amount of technique or hand skill, for we were put to carry out work originated by the draughtsman kept on the premises *to do the designing.* Our training was merely a mechanical one. and what efforts in the direction of original work I made was in the nature of

* Those on Interior Decoration. Glass Painting. Wood Carving. and Pottery Painting.

copying or imitating the work I was put to trace. Glass-painting itself at the time of which I am speaking was governed by precedent. It was purely a conventional art following a path in which the same old ruts had deepened year by year; and the idea of developing the indivi-duality of the craftsmen, so that a touch of originality was seen in what was produced, was an idea too antagonistic to the established order of things for the " firm " to enter-tain. The art crafts were then carried on so much as trades that the art was crushed out by the combined weight of the ledger and the mechanical routine of the establish-ment.

By the light of my experience I consider that craftsmen have now a very fair prospect before them. In the days of my apprenticeship the work was made so mechanical that the "hands" became machines, and the main interest in their work turned upon Saturday's wages. Now, any man of ideas and personality has the opportunity of getting a hearing and giving his *ego* utterance.

The training I obtained at the West London School of Art was of a very rule-of-thumb character—drawing from uninteresting casts in a heated, fetid underground cellar, where the tuition, meagre as it was, was of as mechanical a character as the work during the day, and so deadening was it that after awhile I dropped going to the school. During my pupilage I developed a certain amount of technical facility, but I was sadly deficient in knowledge of form. I used to trace glass quarries from patterns supplied by one of the firm who was clever at originating quaint birds, animals, &c., and combining them with convention-alised foliage, but over and over again I was called upon to do work greatly in advance of my knowledge. It was like reciting in a language one did not understand.

When I gained more leisure, which was only after I

Fig. 6.

started on my own account working for the trade. I worked constantly from nature, making drawings of plants when I could get away from London, or in the Botanic Gardens, for which place I obtained a student's ticket, and of animal life in the Zoo, for which I have, on and off, had a student's ticket for twenty years. The result of this study of nature upon me was curious. I had while in the glass-painter's employ been trained to see things in a conventional way, suggested partly by Japanese and partly by Gothic work—a blend which the leading designer had discovered for himself and employed with considerable effect. But the study of nature made me revolt against the conventions I had hitherto accepted as the necessary conditions of

Fig. 7.

decorative art, and I went to the other extreme of naturalism. I drew a plant as faithfully as I could, and to adapt it to the decoration of a tile, or vase, or glass quarry, was to use it pretty much as I sketched it. The method of designing as taught in schools of art and inculcated in certain works on plant form as applied to design got little further than arranging plants on a geometrical basis, and this direction given to one's studies added to my own tendencies led me, I consider, astray for some years. There is nothing loses so much time or is so disheartening as having to retrace one's steps owing to being wrongly directed, and I am led to make these personal statements to try and help others by showing them what to avoid.

At this time, too, I worked for a designer whose style

captivated me, and I became a weak reflection of him when I
attempted original work. It is as natural as it is common
that a young man should become enamoured of the work of
a particular artist, and consciously or unconsciously copy it :
no harm follows this if the tendency is kept in check by
other influences at work, but to become the pupil of one
man, however clever he may be, is harmful. It checks
originality, the development of the ego ; and the positive
good that the study of another man's work brings is nullified

SYRINGA

Fig. 8.

by the mannerism one falls into. Were I advising a pupil
I should recommend him to study all classes of work which
had a marked individuality and strongly imbued with the
artist's self, making notes of their several characteristics and
even working on the suggestions received. Stevenson tells
us that to acquire the style which has made him one of the
forces in literature he turned over in his mind any sentence
he came across which he considered excellent, and he even
tried to write a sentence with the same cadence in it or
turn of expression. This gave him both facility and an

ear for the music of words—that haunting quality which his choice of words and phrasing give his best writings. The designer can apply the same method to his work that Stevenson did to his, but let your models be many, and so far as your self criticism allows, be certain that the examples you select to study are possessed of lasting qualities, and have not a merely meretricious attraction.

It will be gathered that training the student in what is termed a particular "style" of design (Louis XV., for example) is to put him entirely on the wrong scent, or, to use my former simile, is teaching him to speak in a language he does not understand, as a parrot is taught to chatter. Style *is* individuality, and all training should be in the direction of developing the ego ; but simple as this reads, it was many years before such knowledge became part of my equipment, and therefore of any use to me. I fell first of all under glass-painters' Gothic ; then under Japanese ; after that German Renaissance, largely because my early training had not taught me that individuality was what is demanded of one, and that these so-called styles are merely the crystallising into rigid forms of the work of some strong personality which weak natures force upon one as the decalogue was upon the Jews ; whereas every worker should think and act for himself, and be taught that there are, as Kipling says of tribal lays, nine-and-sixty ways of writing them. Rules and canons of art are at best only aphorisms, and not dogmas, which to disobey is to be artistically lost.

Nothing so corrects the tendency to become the slave of some man's work as a study of nature. It takes one back to first principles, it pulls against the bias another's personality exerts upon one, it refreshes the mind and keeps one's work vigorous and veracious. Nothing gives one so much facility as drawing plant form, both in designing and working, and my impression is that every craftsman would find it pay him to give a day a week to making studies for certainly half the year. One settles down to one's work, gets busy, and then one is tempted to work from the same old studies time after time; whereas if we constantly made fresh studies, our minds would be always on the

Fig. 9.

alert, receiving fresh hints and suggestions instead of becoming jaded and falling back upon one's own or another's conventions.

In drawing plant form my experience of twenty years tells me that the less you know botanically about plants the better. The artist works from observation rather than knowledge. To paint a field of grass does not depend upon a knowledge of what goes to make the *tout ensemble,* but on an eye trained to appreciate the subtleties of colour and the

power of rendering surfaces. I consider I wasted much
valuable time in making sections of plants, drawing the
internal parts of flowers, and troubling about the physiology
of the herbs I studied. I am speaking here as an artist,
for, of course, botany is an interesting study in itself, but
has nothing to do with design, though some designers, I

BARTONIA

Fig. 10.

doubt not, have received suggestions from botanical sections.
I made the outline studies accompanying these notes during
the intervals of putting this chapter into shape, just to
show my readers the sort of nature-notes I find useful, as
well as to illustrate some of the ideas I have put down
here, and I made them as they grew in the garden.
There is a great gain in this, for you study the general

growth of the plant itself, and the most valuable suggestions come to one of lines and angles and curves by drawing from the growing plant. If you pick off a spray and put it in a vase and draw it, you may miss the very thing that is of

CUP & SAUCER
HARE-
    BELL

SWEET PEA

AQUILEGIA

DIELYTRA

Fig. 11.

value as a decorative suggestion. Besides, while making your drawing you are led to observe the plant much more attentively, and your eye is directed to its "points," which is not the case if you merely take it in generally. In fact, you never can say you begin to know a plant until you have drawn it, and you may draw it many times before *the* suggestion which is of value comes to you. A study you make yourself is consequently of far more value than one of another's, because you dwell upon that in a plant which touches your bias, and your own drawing, therefore, speaks to you in a way that one obtained second hand never can.

The four studies of thistle, meadow-sweet, cow-parsley, and figwort were portions of the illustrations accompanying an article I contributed to *The Art Journal* some years ago on "Hedgerow Decoration." They are literal transcripts of nature of plants which it seems to me to have special significance to a designer, and they also emphasise what I said just now about drawing by observation instead of botanically.

Many books on plant form have been issued, and I do not deny their use, but the plant itself is only a means to the end, and not the end itself, and therefore nothing takes the place of original observation. A design is not necessarily the conventional rendering of a particular plant, but the ideas of line, mass, and distribution which the plant suggests.

The form of leaf known as "Acanthus" crops up again and again, for craftsmen, from Greek times until now, have seen the beauty in a long deeply serrated leaf curving outwards, and partially wrapped around the main stem, but instead of working on an old suggestion, would it not be more profitable to go out and make a study of the opium poppy, and try and import a touch of originality into the design you base upon it?

The oriental poppy, again, is full of decorative hints.

The cup-like form of the leaves around the main stem I

Fig. 12.

could conceive being a fruitful suggestion to a worker in

c

Meadow
Sweet
in Seed
August

Fig. 13.

metal or wrought iron. Particular attention should always

Fig. 14.

be paid to the angle the leaf makes with the stem. The

Fig. 15.

weakness of a design is more often manifest in this than in any other thing, and the infinite variety in nature in the angle made by the leaf with the stem leaves a designer no excuse for such weakness.

The study of curves is one that a designer should specially direct his attention to. Tendrils, as those of the vine, afford a wonderful play of line, and might be studied with advantage. Their eccentricity teaches one how dependent on nature one is, for, try and invent an eccentric line, and you will be astonished at the limited range of your fancy. The nasturtium, again, is in this respect interesting, and the habit the leaves have of curling themselves around the stems might be often worked upon.

Truth to nature is not

fidelity to the characteristics of a particular plant, but the doing of nothing that is contrary to the principles of plant growth. A design may be so sublimated as to suggest no plant in particular, and yet be perfectly true in the relation of its parts ; and this truthfulness can only come by saturating yourself with knowledge derived by observation.

It is not necessary to write anything specially about each of these plant studies. It is enough to say that I believe in drawing each plant with scrupulous exactitude and just as it appears, rather than a conventional rendering of it. More subtlety of line and crispness of touch is likely to be seen in work where a reverential truthfulness characterises the nature notes. Exercise your power of selection not only in the plants you study, but also in the portions sketched, and be sure to endeavour

Fig. 16. - Drawing of Lilium Auratum. By Kifu Rissho.

to catch the characteristics of each plant. The two studies by Rissho and Hokusai will direct the student's attention to Japanese work, especially the masterly yet simple way Japanese artists draw from nature. No craftsman can afford to neglect Japanese art.

Go for at least one thing in each study—the twist of a

tendril, the curve of a stem, the growth of leaf from stem,
or whatever it may be which strikes you as material worth
preserving for future work ; and it is not sufficient to
make a batch of studies and think you have enough to
last you all your days.

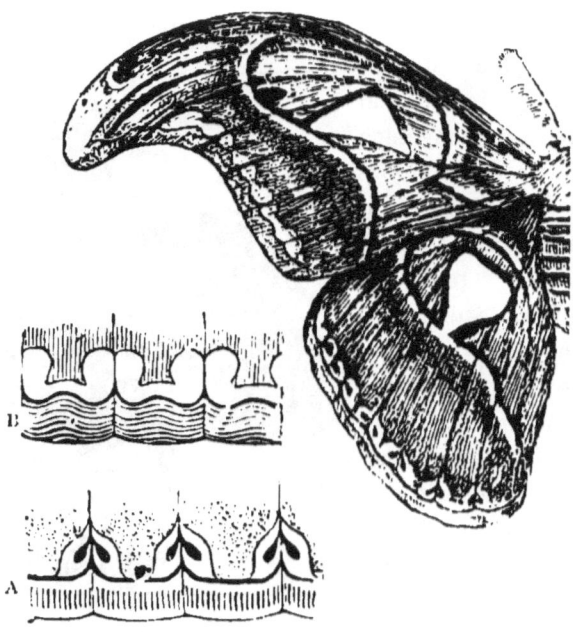

Fig. 17 — Great Atlas Moth.
The ornamental borders A and B are derived from the wings of this moth.

Drawing from nature should be an important part of
the training of a craftsman, and he should constantly
study her, for you never can say you have learnt a plant.
Fresh suggestions may come to you, and that after you
think you have got to know the plant by heart. Nothing

so refreshes the mind, and prevents that jaded mechanical look work is apt to get when one works on year after year without seeking fresh impulses from nature, as studying nature.

Plant form, though the most important source of inspiration to the craftsman, is not the only one. A bird's wing, a feather, the marking on the wings of a butterfly, as in Fig. 17, may supply valuable hints; in fact, it is hard to say when the mind is on the alert what does not stimulate it.

I have avoided attempting to show how any of the plants I have sketched may be adapted, though many writers have done so, as I hold that each worker has to do this for himself. There is no one way, and I don't wish to thrust my point of view upon the student.

Fig. 17A. Study of Lily. By Hokusai

CHAPTER II.

DESIGN AND CRAFTSMANSHIP.

THE two are one, and should be indivisible, for no craftsman can be full statured who is not an artist, and no designer can succeed in applied art who is not something of a craftsman, and for this reason. You must know what are the particular qualities to be brought out in each craft before you can design for it. We will assume that you are going to use the Oriental poppy as the *motif*, and it has to be adapted to three different purposes —a repoussé cup, a painted tile, and a piece of embroidery. Now, it might be imagined that to make one design would be sufficient, and that it could be used with slight modifications for the three crafts. As a matter of fact, that is what would have been done in my apprenticeship days, for anything was good enough *then* for decorative art; but now that the art crafts have been recognised as taking quite as high a place in man's handiwork as any other art (so-called *fine*), a more reasonable practice is followed, and the student beating a cup would seize upon certain characteristics of the poppy because the beaten metal will render some feature of the poppy better than could be obtained by a painted tile, while the embroiderer, again, would develop some other characteristic of the plant to

suit the requirements of his work. The first thing, therefore, is to study the requirements of your craft, so that you
may develop them to the utmost, and your design is
therefore conditioned by the necessity of bringing out the
qualities of the material you work in.

Let us look at the matter a little closer. In repoussé
work your effect is produced by beating some parts of the
metal in high relief, and throwing others back, and this
breaking up of the surface to produce light and shade is
the first and chief point to be aimed at. Now, an oriental
poppy has a hairy surface, but this is a peculiarity which
the metal-worker can hardly, if at all, take into account,
because beaten metal would not be helped by having the
surface broken up minutely to give the effect of hair: it is
a feature of the plant he can afford to ignore. But the tile
painter might easily hint at the hairy surface if he chose to,
because he is using a much more flexible material than the
metal-worker—one in which greater delicacy of manipulation is possible. The embroiderer, again, has a much less
flexible material to deal with than the tile-painter. To
obtain the effect of roundness or relief is almost an impossibility, or, at all events, would be a matter of excessive
labour, out of all proportion to the effect produced, and
further, embroidery does not depend for its effect upon the
quality we find in repoussé work, but upon a pleasing disposition of lines where form is only hinted at and not
simulated.

It will be noticed that I have been assuming that one
man is called upon to make designs for three different
crafts, not necessarily for himself to carry out ; on the contrary, the work is split up between two classes of workers,

the design being the work of one and the execution of
another.   This is making the worker a mere finger machine,
and the designer the so-called thinking machine, and is
just what we want to avoid.   The craftsman should be his
own designer ; in fact, design should be developed out of
finger dexterity.   To show his skill as a metal-worker, and
his appreciation of the quality of the material he works in,
should suggest the design.   The relationship is so *intime*
between the material and the design wrought upon it that
the two are, as I said at the beginning of this chapter, one,
and should be indissoluble.   It is practically impossible to
make a design on paper, say, for a repoussé cup, which shall
bear any close relationship to the cup when beaten, and
even a design for embroidery bears only a slight affinity to
the same when wrought with the needle, for a line on paper
has none of the value of the same made up of stitches on a
woven surface ; and unless this is borne in mind, the apparent poverty of a working design induces the designer to
endeavour to obtain richness by elaborating the design on
paper, with the result that, when carried out, the work is
wanting in simplicity, doesn't seem to fit the material or the
material fit the design, and this because the design is made
independent of the method of reproduction, instead of being
developed out of it.

A student should train himself as a designer at the
same time that he is acquiring the *techne* of his craft, and
there should never be a time when the one is thought more
of than the other, for the reason I have given that the two
play into each other and do not exist separately.   This is
no arbitrary statement, for if we consider the matter, the
tyro has so limited an amount of skill that only a very simple

design can be attempted by him, but as his hand cunning increases, his desire for more elaborate work will manifest itself; and though it may take a wrong direction at times and lead him to do what should never be attempted, he will by degrees learn the class of effect his material most adequately renders, and within the conditions imposed upon him by his craft work to the best end.

It is some time before the student sets the full value upon his material and directs his energies to developing its particular qualities. In this connection I may mention that in my early days as a glass painter I was shown on one occasion a highly naturalesque piece of glass-painting. It was a head after Guido, and looked not unlike an indifferent oleograph. I had hitherto only seen glass painted in the severe manner of the fourteenth century, and this rococo piece of glass painting delighted me because it looked *so much like a picture.* No reason was given me why this highly enamelled glass picture was not worthy the praise I bestowed on it. I was merely snubbed and laughed at for admiring it, whereas, had it been pointed out to me that to attempt to paint a picture on glass was putting the material to the worst possible use, and was not developing its resources, but, on the contrary, was doing quite the opposite, it would have saved me some misdirected energy later on. It is the duty of the teacher to direct the student's attention quite as much to what is most worth doing as it is how best to do it, and this should be done by appealing to the student's reason rather than by sneering at his prejudices. The student can be helped, too, by being shown good examples of old and modern work in which the resources of the particular craft are developed on right

lines. As to what these right lines are the following chapters
will make some attempt at showing.

How entirely design is controlled by method of reproduction is seen in the economy of means to end. Human
labour is a valuable thing, and should be highly prized and
reverently and economically employed. To use it inade-
quately by misdirecting it or undervaluing it is thriftlessness
or worse. A designer unacquainted with the technique of
the craft he essays to work for is almost certain to fall into
one or both errors. I hold strongly that the maximum of
effect should be produced with the minimum of effort.
Craftsmanship is the result of a series of well-directed single
efforts, each representing so much physical and mental
power. Each of these efforts, therefore, should be valued,
so that no waste takes place, and the beauty of hand labour
is seen largely in the "trick of the tool's true play." Machine work cannot have this, as a machine can only fac-
simile a particular piece of work the required number of
times. It can therefore secure you great accuracy, and give
you work which is "faultily faultless, icily regular, splendidly
null." It were surely wrong, therefore, to try to make
machinery give you the nervous irregularity of the hand as
to put the hand to do what a machine so unerringly accom-
plishes. These remarks are truisms I know, and yet how
constantly we see them disregarded. It is only quite
recently that the beauty of beaten silver in spoons, for
instance, has been recognised, simply because our eyes had
grown accustomed to the highly polished surface which we
grew to think indispensable to plate. Habit and custom
largely govern taste, because so few of us think indepen-
dently and act for ourselves. Yet it is in the breaking

away from the established order of things that our personality finds expression, and an original turn is given to work. You use tradition and are guided by precedent, but are not bounded by it. You must avail yourself of the past or you get no further than the painted mask outside a wig-

Fig. 18.

wam, but from what is known and has been accomplished you stretch out to the unknown and reach forward to that which is waiting for you to do.

Mr. George Frampton put this to me very graphically by roughly sketching on the back of a letter the two

Fig. 19.

diagrams I have redrawn, as they better explain what one means than many words. You have a long narrow space to decorate, let us say. One very familiar plan is to have an undulating line with scrolls springing from it, and flowers and leaves to fill up Fig. 18). The man who first hit upon this certainly succeeded in filling his space in a very admirable

way : so admirable, indeed, that many of us have not
troubled to think out any other way, but content ourselves
with small modifications of it.   But a craftsman might

Fig. 20.   Portion of Mitchell Memorial.   By G. Frampton, A.R.A.

come along who, disregarding this scrolly arrangement,
took two such well-known forms as the cabbage and daisy,
and, arranging them something as in Fig. 19, broke away at

once from tradition, and showed us that there was one other way at least of decorating a long narrow space.

The same sculptor, referring to a memorial to Mitchell, the shipbuilder, which he was working at the last time I was in his *atelier*, told me that people have grown so accus-

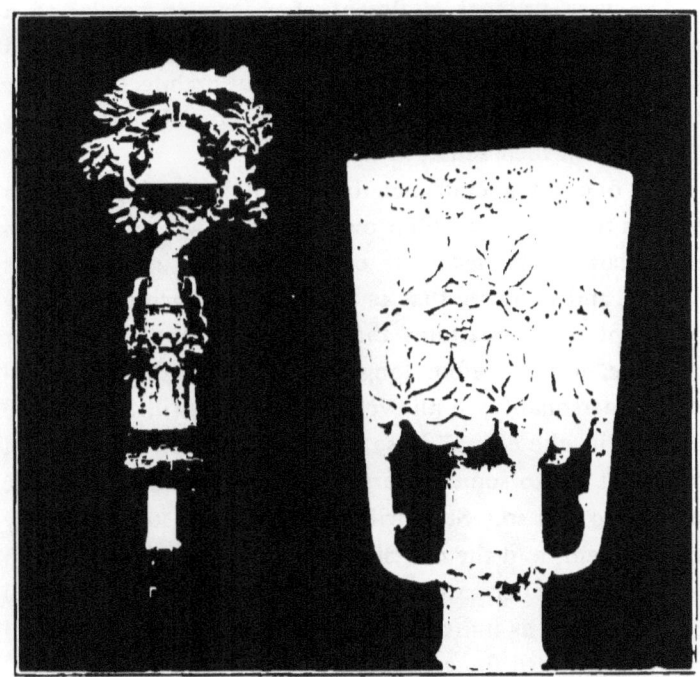

Fig. 21. Carved Wood Capital and Crozier in Metal.
By G. Frampton, A.R.A.

tomed to pillars and capitals in architecture, that when he divided his panels with conventionalised tree trunks and foliage, they felt almost outraged, and one architect expostulated with him on the enormity of his proceeding. Yet because pillars have been used for so many centuries, it does not follow that there is no other way of supporting an arch or dividing a series of architectural spaces or niches, and yet the man who breaks away from tradition is certain to bring down a storm of criticism upon him from those who cannot open their minds to a new impression.

The very original treatment of a wooden capital to a pillar in the handsome fire-place exhibited at the "Arts and Crafts" in 1896 was condemned by some architects, because it did not follow custom or conform to rule—was not a "capital" in their sense, in fact !

The one thing craftsmen have to fight for is liberty to express themselves in their own way. It will take time to effect, but events hasten at certain periods in the world's history, and I foresee that as the public is much more ready to accept new departures than it was in the days of my pupilage, it will before long demand originality, or, at all events, personality, in all work : the crafts will have to be steeped in the ego of those who wrought them, instead of being cut out to some pattern which custom has termed the style of so and so. Style will not then mean some arbitrary arrangement, and the craftsman treated as a piece of cloth pinned to a paper pattern by which to shape him, but will be recognised as individuality, the expression of a trained mind and skilled fingers rejoicing in its work.

That division of art into "Fine" and that which is not fine is of course a wholly misleading one, and shows a great lack of appreciation as to what constitutes art on the part of those who make such a division. No such distinction can be made, for the same impulses are stirred, whether you paint a portrait or carve a pew end. Thought, imagination, an eye for proportion, hand cunning, the result of long training, are required wherever art is produced. The artist should throw himself just as strongly into his work, whether he choose to carve, work in metal, or paint on canvas. The idea that anything will do because the work is not bounded by a gilt frame is happily dying out. There is no higher or lower art ; it is all to be judged from the same platform. As Ruskin says, "The only essential distinction between decorative and other art is the being fitted for a fixed place ; and in that place, related, either in subordination or in command, to the effect of other pieces of art. And all the greatest art which the world has produced is thus fitted for a place, and subordinated to a purpose. There is no existing highest order art but is decorative. The best sculpture yet produced has been the decoration of a temple front—the best painting the decoration of a room."

The tendency to specialisation which comes of the subdivision of work in these days is very detrimental to the development of a craftsman. Physically, change of work is rest, and an artist tired of one work can by change of labour achieve what idleness cannot. The great men of the past did everything in their calling, and some of the marked personalities in the present day are all-round workers. Witness, Alfred Gilbert, George Frampton, and Alex. Fisher, to take three names occurring to me, and the reproductions of the work of the last two in these pages.

Before taking up some of the more prominent art crafts individually, I wish to make it clear to the reader that what follows is not a series of "lessons" on these crafts, but an examination of the principles underlying the successful practice of them, with special reference to the work of

Fig. 22.— Nature Study, modelled in Low Relief by A. Wakeford.
(Prize work, South Kensington.)

modern craftsmen. The only training worth anything is working under a practical man, for technique cannot be imparted successfully by written directions, and training in the art crafts can be obtained much more easily now than it could a few years since. At the end of the book will be found a few of the schools in London where instruction is given in the crafts, with some of the teachers engaged; but instruction in hand-cunning, however thorough it be, is not the only teaching necessary. Work must exhibit taste as well as skill, and harmony between means and end, by which I mean that every craftsman should so work that the utmost is made of the particular quality inherent in each craft. Wood should not be carved as though it were stone, or glass painted as though it were a canvas; and it will be my endeavour to point out what is the direction one's work should take to secure the best results—best, that is, from the point of view of the craft itself, for on the question of " design " dogmatism is *de trop;* besides, what little of a definite nature I have had to say on that subject has already been said.

In the former chapter I have dwelt on the necessity of drawing much from nature. Modelling is also very helpful —in some respects even more helpful. The modelled panel by A. Wakeford is an excellent specimen of work direct from nature, the character of the plant being caught with artistic sympathy.

The chapters which follow will deal with some of the important art crafts, and, being illustrated from the works of some of the best craftsmen of the day, ought, on that ground, to be of use to the student, who can see at a glance in what direction the Art of the day is moving.

CHAPTER III.

REPOUSSÉ AND FINE METAL-WORK.

" He who blows thro' bronze, may breathe thro' silver."

O bring out the beauty of metal it is necessary that some portions should catch the light and others be thrown into shadow, and the more we break up the surface judiciously the more beautiful will be the effect, as we can see by comparing a machine-polished piece of brass and one hammered out, so that each hammer mark shows. And yet for years the public was under the spell of highly polished metal, whether it were ordinary brass work or silver plate. There is a beauty of its own in a piece of beaten silver or copper, and if we add to this a design, no matter how simple it may be, produced by beating up the metal from the back, we have within our reach a beautiful craft, and, in the hands of an artist, one capable of great things. Beaten metal, by reason of this variety of surface a series of facets, one might say) which comes of hammering, seems " to live," while the machine-polished surface by its very perfection acts icily on the senses, and has a dead perfection about it which leaves us untouched. Where we can follow the hand cunning and see the marks of the tool, metal is then made human—we associate it with an individual and are drawn to it.

I put *Repoussé* in the first place as a surface decoration

for metal. So great value does the mere beaten metal give a design, that there is a danger of letting anything do instead of paying the greatest heed to the design you elect to beat up, for if a poor design is enhanced by the method of production, a really beautiful and suitable one is made precious by it,—and metal should always have this quality of preciousness, and this quite apart from the value of the metal itself—a finely worked piece of repoussé steel can certainly possess it as much as silver or gold. Some metals are more beautiful than others, but the value of metal-work should be in the design and workmanship. We see this in old silver, which will, for choice examples, fetch some pounds per oz., though its value as metal is about 2s. 1d. Where expensive metals such as gold or platinum are used, it is obvious that the work must be confined within a limited space, which, therefore, "conditions" the design. Much more delicacy of manipulation can and should be given to a piece of jewellery than would be effective on a dish, say 18 inches in diameter, for it is a truism to say that it is always necessary to keep a due relationship between design and area to be decorated, though it is not always observed.

Seeing that repoussé is finished from the front as well as beaten up at the back, a considerable amount of detail can be wrought in the design, but the effectiveness of repoussé does not depend upon minuteness of manipulation so much as upon a judicious discriminating number of accents or sharp lines, just to help the beaten-up parts. There should be the feeling of a wave— the ebb and flow of the sea—about repoussé. The design should swell up and recede and die away into the metal, and no one part, to my thinking, should be in excessive relief. The plane of the surface should not be destroyed by the decoration, and then there is always the danger of breaking through the metal in the more highly beaten parts, and this with all the care that may be exercised. If this happens, then the part has to be soldered.

A beginner should choose such an article as a door-plate, and confine himself to beating up a few simple forms in low relief, and depend largely upon producing the effect by the

Fig. 23.— Silver Casket designed by G. Frampton, A.R.A., for the Skinners' Company.

beating up from the back. Avoid imitating nature. Think of treating metal effectively rather than rendering objects.

Silver and copper are the metals most usually employed. Silver beats well and has a beautiful frosted appearance, quite different to the highly polished metal we call plate. It was a revelation to many people at the Arts and Crafts Exhibitions to see beaten silver spoons and dishes, for the metal looks infinitely more valuable than polished silver. For jewellery, too, silver is very appropriate, and specimens of repoussé jewellery are given in the chapter on that subject.

Copper for all general purposes is the best metal to beat, being tough and elastic. Brass is more brittle and is little used.

Steel is used for small work, and Mr. Alex. Fisher has worked in this metal with beautiful results. So, too, has Mr. Nelson Dawson.

Pewter is sometimes used, and I have seen it effectively employed in some electric light fittings by Mr. Ashbee.

I cannot do better, for the encouragement of those who have yet to "find" themselves, than give a few personal notes about some of the craftsmen whose work is figured in these pages.

The experiences of Mr. Nelson Dawson and Mr. Catterson-

Fig. 24 - Emu's Egg Centrepiece, with Beaten and Cast Metal Supports. By Nelson Dawson.

Smith point to the conclusion that if one art calling will not receive the earnest worker, another may offer him the opportunity he desires of giving his aspirations utterance. Mr. Gilbert Marks again, who was, when I wrote about him in *The Art Journal*, only devoting his leisure to metal-

work, has received sufficient encouragement to throw up
the commercial bird in the hand for the artistic two in the
bush.

Mr. Nelson Dawson is an instance of a man who has
experimented for some time before he finds out what it
would appear he can best do. From architecture he turned
his attention to painting, and his water-colour studies of
the sea evince observation, selection, and high technical
skill, as those who have seen his work in the Royal Academy
and British Artists, and other galleries, know. But Mr.
Dawson experienced what so many painters have done, or
are doing, that the patronage extended to the painter of
pictures is meagre in the extreme. The world, apparently,
can, all too easily for artists, do without pictures ; and what
is more degrading than to spend half your energy in fruit-
lessly trying to secure purchasers for your handiwork ?
There is a story told of Flateau, the eminent picture dealer
of the forties and fifties, who met Dickens at dinner. After
hearing every one talking about the novelist's cleverness for
some time, he turned to his neighbour and said, " I dare say
he's a good writer, but *I* call it clever to make a man buy a
picture as doesn't want to." Mr. Dawson began hammering metal as a pastime, and finding that he could express
himself in this way, took it up more seriously, until com-
missions began to come in, and now he has, in addition to
his own atelier, workshops for more distinctly commercial
work, like hinges and door-plates.

My first acquaintance with Mr. Nelson Dawson's metal-
work were some hammered door-plates he did for a few
of his artist neighbours at Chelsea. It was impossible to
avoid noticing them because they were so fresh and dis-

tinctive. One did not realise what could be made of a

Fig. 25. Sketch of Centrepiece in Silver and Gilt, parts Enamelled.
Design Modelled and Chased by Alex. Fisher, and Exhibited at
the Royal Academy, June, 1897.

door posts until one saw what Mr. Dawson made of them.

and having seen we wondered how it was that it had been
left to one man to point out the more excellent way.

Mr. Nelson Dawson, whose studio is in Manresa Road,
Chelsea, told me that he found his training as an architect
useful to him now that he had become an Art craftsman,

but the greatest help he received
was from his wife. " If it were not
for Mrs. Dawson it would have
been impossible for me to have
taken up enamelling as I have
done. In fact, it is more her work
than mine," he said.

Mr. Dawson, like Mr. Fisher,
who taught the former enamelling.
uses enamels a good deal in his
metal-work.

Though beaten metal-work first
engaged his attention. he does not
confine himself to copper or silver,
for I saw some highly ornamental
hinges made for a hanging cabinet
of beaten steel, but I am unable to
give a drawing of them here, as

Fig. 26. - Hand - Mirror
Back. Designed and
executed by Alex. Fisher.

Mr. Dawson finds that in the
commercial work turned out under
his direction—he has a regular

workshop in which his designs are carried out under his
supervision—his designs get copied (always very badly) by
" the Firms." A memorial tablet of repoussé copper gave
me some idea of how taste and thought can give value to
a work otherwise of no special interest.

Mr. Alexander Fisher was a National scholar some ten years ago, having come from Torquay to London on obtaining his scholarship. The student, following in his

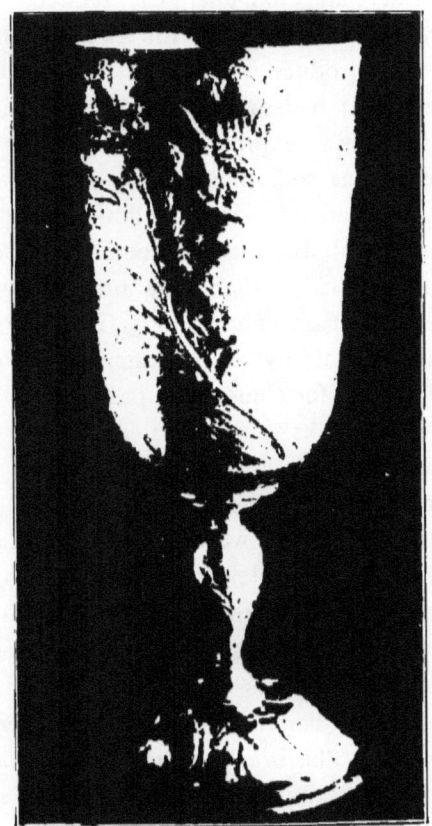

Fig. 27. Cup. By Gilbert Marks.

father's footsteps at that time, was an enameller on pottery, but while at Kensington, having taken up enamelling on metal, his attention was naturally turned to metal-work itself. To an artist-craftsman it would seem an unnecessary subdivision of labour for one to do the metal-work and another enamel it. The fact that Mr. Fisher has won a name as an enameller has tended to obscure his work in fine metal; but the two sketches he has allowed me to reproduce, as well as the mirror, is ample evidence, were that necessary, that we have here an artist whose ambition it is to express himself in his own way, and, what is more, he has something to say as well as the skill to say it. Like that old master Cellini, enamelling comes largely into play in Mr. Fisher's metal-work, and a very beautiful adjunct it is. I shall have more to say about Mr. Fisher in the chapter on enamelling. The Royal Academy has recognised his ability as a craftsman by giving prominence to his work for some years past.

In Mr. Gilbert Marks' case his talent would appear to be hereditary, for he is the grandson of a working goldsmith as well as the nephew of the late Fred Walker and H. S. Marks, R.A. His metal-work, which is chiefly beaten silver, was the work of his leisure (helped by two assistants), for Mr. Marks was "something in the City," though now Art wholly claims him for her own. A bold free treatment of plant form characterises Mr. Marks' design, the metal and the method of hammering it entirely governing this part of his work. The breaking up of the surface so as to get lights and darks is the first consideration in repoussé, and I am glad to see that Mr. Marks understands the value of breadth in his designs, and avoids producing his effect by the aggregation of "small" *motifs*, but keeps his work large and simple. The silver casket, Fig. 23, designed by Mr. G. Frampton, was executed by Mr. Marks.

Mr. Catterson-Smith came from Dublin in 1874 to be under Foley, but the Royal Academician dying soon after, Mr. Smith took up painting, and it was not until 1892 that he turned his attention to metal-work. He said to me, " I

Fig. 28. Dish of Beaten Silver. By R. Catterson-Smith.

only wish some good angel had advised me to adopt the metal craft twenty years ago. I believe the salvation of Art and artists lies in the Art crafts."

What instruction in craftsmanship he received was at the Bedford Park School of Art, which is close to his house,

and what proficiency he has attained is the result of
his own endeavour.   I am able to give, in Fig. 28,
a repoussé silver salver beaten out of the flat by Mr.
Catterson-Smith, which is an excellent specimen of plant
form adapted to decorative purposes.   A London firm,

Fig. 29.—Alms-Dish of Cast and Chased Silver.
By Arthur G. Walker.

who sold some of Mr. Smith's work, tried to get their own
workmen to reproduce this particular salver, but without
success; for the men, being trained as mechanics, could
not give the work that freedom and spontaneity which gives
beaten metal its "preciousness."   They tried to copy

painstakingly what was largely the result of accident, and, as one may imagine, only failure was the result.

The silver alms-dish, by Mr. Arthur Walker, was bought

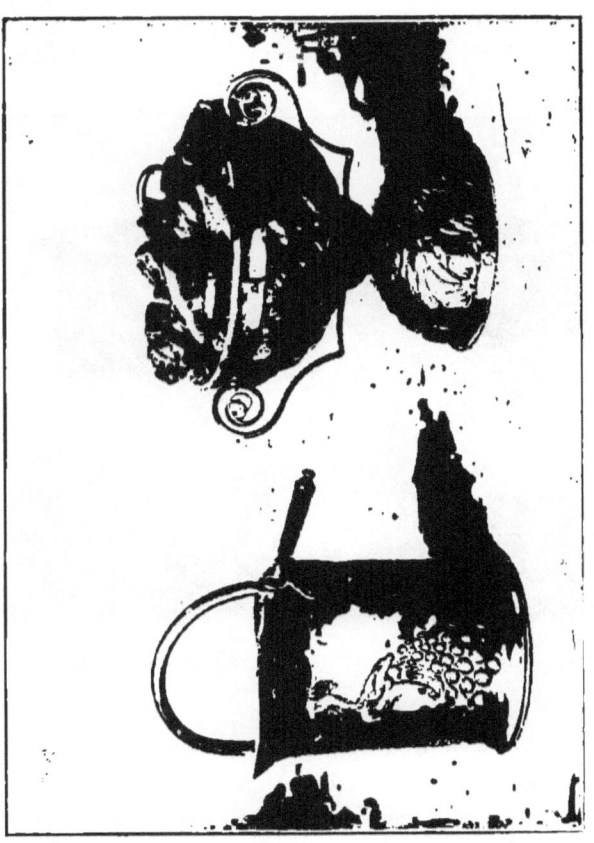

Fig. 30.—Beaten Copper Coal Vase.   Designed by C. R. Ashbee.

by Mr. Thompson Yates from the Academy some three years ago. It is cast and chased, but the details are much lost in the reproduction, though it is an excellent piece of work.

The purchaser has recently presented it to a church near
Liverpool.

Mr. Ashbee's name is linked with the work carried on
at Essex House, Mile End, where everything from a coal-
scuttle to a mantelpiece is made. His object is to supply a
house with all the furniture—using this word in its widest

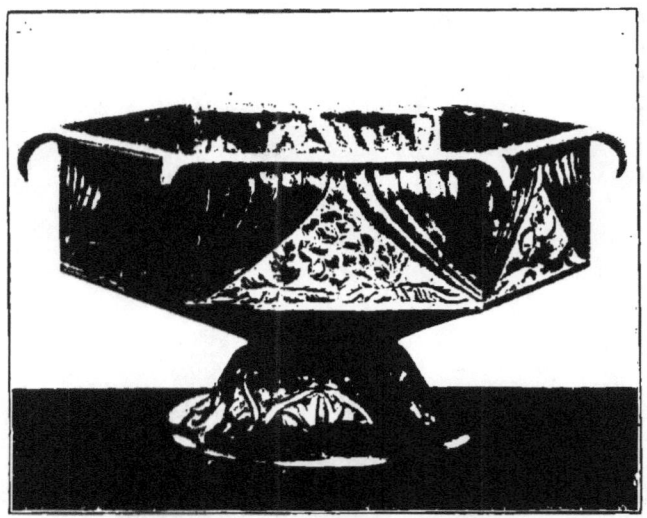

Fig. 31.—Jardinière in Repoussé Copper. (Chiswick School of
Arts and Crafts.)

sense—that is required in it. The beaten copper coal
vase is a good example of what such work should be.

Mr. Ashbee has given some attention to jewellery and
silver work, specimens of which will be given in the chapter
on jewellery.

Mr. George Frampton, A.R.A., has allowed me to repro-
produce a silver casket which he designed for the Skinners'

Company. It is an entirely frank piece of work, as the rivets show. Why cannot those who have the giving of prizes, which take the form of plate, patronise an artist instead of a manufacturer? I know men who have been successful sportsmen who have innumerable cups won in

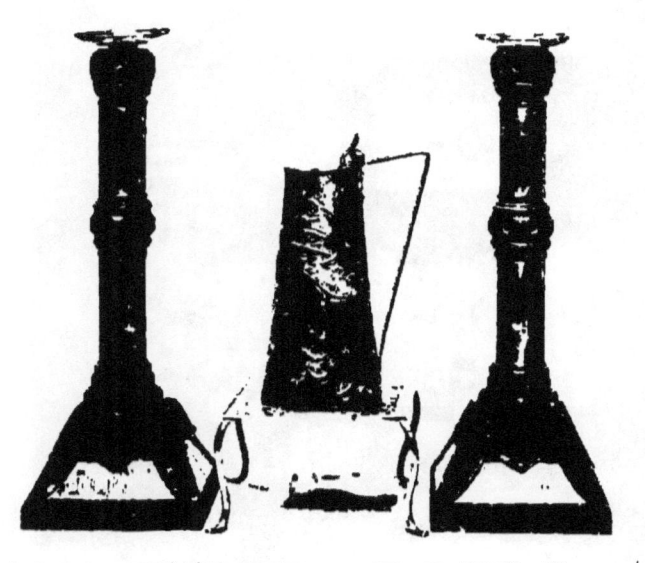

Fig. 32. Altar Candlesticks in Oak and Gun Metal, and Hot-Water Jug in Repoussé Copper. Keswick School of Industrial Arts.)

competitions, which are neither useful nor ornamental. They stow them away in cases, and, except for their value as metal, are worthless. There is any amount of talent waiting to be employed in metal-work, and it rests therefore with the patron if something better than the ordinary cup or vase is not competed for.

The Birmingham Guild of Handicraft is an association of craftsmen working in all departments of skilled labour. The finger-plates, handles, and other articles of everyday

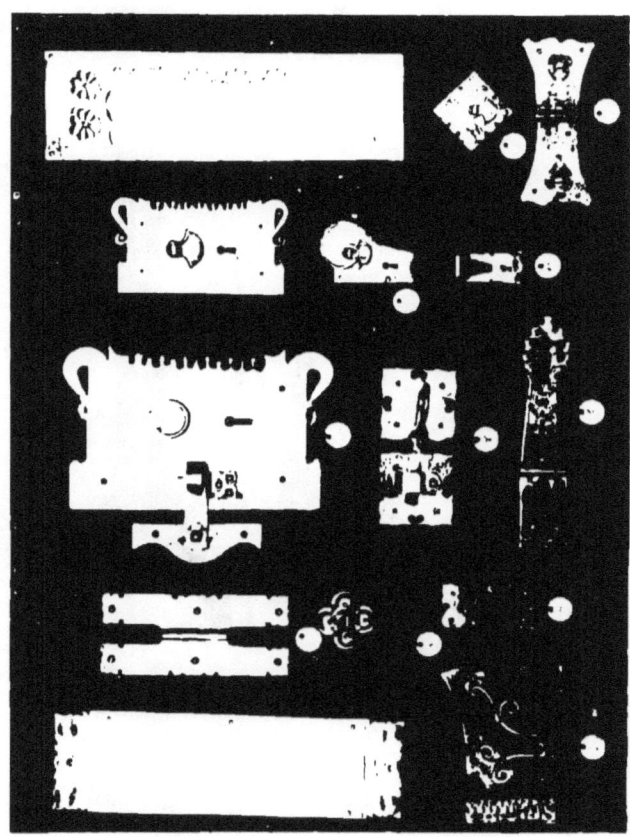

Fig. 35.—Commercial Metal-Work.   By the Birmingham Guild of Handicraft.

utility show that this guild is grappling with the difficulty of bringing Art into common life, for it is useless holding abstract, academic views on what should be : the thing is

to do something which will soon lead to the more excellent
way, and this the Guild of Handicraft is doing. It is by
taking in hand the ordinary "furniture" of life, and making
that of interest and beauty, that commercial success at all
events is to be reached. The word "Brummagem" has
been so long a term of reproach where anything like
artistic work is concerned, that it is pleasant to be able
to bring into notice this Birmingham guild, for though
in "Brum," they are not of it in
spirit, their endeavour being to give
as much Art for the money as
Caleb Plummer did to his toy-horses
for sixpence.

The Birmingham School of Art
is in the front rank as a teaching
institution, and very excellent and
"up-to-date" artistic work emanates
from it. The students seem more
anxious to become art workers than
painters of second or third rate
pictures, and I should say that

Fig. 34.— Design for a Lock Plate. By H. S. Stromquist.

many of them will have no cause to regret this decision.

.   .   .   .   .

I can hear it said that we cannot all have coal-boxes of
hammered copper, or spoons of beaten silver, but then it is
not my purpose to do more than direct the reader's attention to what is being done here and there in craftsmanship,
and not what is generally possible. Art has nothing to do
with economies; besides, the dealer in Tottenham Court
Road is touched by the ebb and flow of tendency in due

course, and will, because one man invests a coal-box with "artistic merit," offer to the *oi polloi* a daintier coal-box than he thought of doing aforetime.

ECCLESIASTICAL METAL-WORK.

When Solomon built the Temple we are told that he sent to the King of Tyre for "a man cunning to work in gold, and in silver, and in brass, and in iron," and Hiram sent Solomon a cunning man, "endued with understanding, who could grave any manner of graving, and could find out every device that was put to him." It cannot be said that those who build Temples in this land take the trouble to search out the cunning workers, or we should not see such lamentable waste of money in our religious buildings that so often makes the judicious grieve.

It is a great pleasure, therefore, to be able to give examples of the ecclesiastical metal-work of two men who are doing their best to raise the standard of church work. It is a poor commentary on the Art education of the clergy that so little support is given to artists who are waiting to be hired to devote their energies and talents to the decoration of our churches. The "firm" and manufacturer is constantly chosen, and the individual left to eat his heart out with disappointment for lack of encouragement.

A glance at the work of H. Wilson and W. Bainbridge Reynolds shows how excellent is the effect obtainable by treating metal either as a surface to be beaten up, hammered, and made to lose and find itself as in the example by the former, Fig. 35, or where metal is twisted and pulled into a succession of geometrically planned *motifs*, the whole form-

Fig. 35.—Door. By H. Wilson.

ing a coherent, logically built-up design, as in Mr. Reynolds'

screen, Fig. 36, here illustrated. Mr. Wilson would appear
to be less influenced by tradition than Mr. Reynolds, for
while the latter works in the Gothic spirit, Mr. Wilson may
be said to be expressing his ego regardless of what the craftsmen of the middle ages have done. I am not in any way
instituting a comparison between these two nineteenth-
century craftsmen. I merely desire to see each man's work
from his own point of view, for the work speaks for itself.
The craftsmen shall speak for themselves.

Mr. Wilson's work in metal, for he, like Mr. Reynolds,
is an architect as well as craftsman, has so far been mostly
confined to repoussé copper and brass in the form of door
sheathing, panels for fireplaces and chimney breasts,
though he has in hand some candelabra and other
work. Mr. Wilson said to me that he wished to avoid
altogether any reminiscence of traditional habits or manners
of design, and he therefore goes direct to nature and
endeavours to realise in his work that spirit which the study
of natural form suggests, and in his designs to suggest the
spring and growth of natural forms instead of those conventions which, like precedents in law, so many designers
are content to abide by. If men worked in this spirit we
should hear no more about the style of Louis XIV. or any
other period, but the expression of the individual.

It is evident that Mr. Wilson feels very strongly on this
point, for he says:—" I can never understand that attitude
of mind which makes men content to reproduce variations
of other men's work, even though the men whose work is
copied lived in the heroic ages. To accept another's
convention is the worst form of intellectual cowardice.

" If we have any vision at all, one's view of things must

Fig. 36.—Screen. By W. Bainbridge Reynolds.

be different from and to that extent interesting, because
it gives us a new conception all others : whereas, any copy
of another man's idea is, at the best, the shadow of a shade,
weaker by one remove at least from that nature which gives
strength to all the best work."

Several examples of Mr. Wilson's work were in the last
Arts and Crafts, among them the brass door of which an
illustration is given.

W. Bainbridge Reynolds was an articled pupil of Mr.
J. D. Seddon, the well-known architect. Soon after he
had completed his articles he worked under the late G. E.
Street, R.A., and it was whilst working on the details
of the iron-work of the new Law Courts that he became
interested in architectural metal-work. He felt, however,
that, although the mediæval tradition in stone and wood-
work had at that time been admirably revived in English
architecture, metal-work was on the whole below the artistic
standard of the best existing examples of old work. He
therefore devoted himself for some years to the study, not
only of mediæval iron-work, but of metal-work in its many
applications, of later periods and of various countries.
Eventually he started, a few years ago, forges and workshops,
where architects' designs in metal, and his own, have been
since executed under his direction.

Mr. Reynolds' principal aim is to consider the forms in
his designs with reference to the particular methods by
which each metal can be worked, and in execution to allow
to be apparent the *human* element, an element which is lost
where the first consideration is a mechanical perfection of
surface. In these days it is all too easy to attain this geometrical precision of form and surface, while to preserve

the "individuality" both of the metal and of the craftsman

Fig. 37. Lectern. By W. Bainbridge Reynolds.

requires an artist's guidance as well as an artist's hand.

The large candelabra was exhibited at the Arts and Crafts in 1886, and, apart from its size, was a noble piece of work.   The riveting together of beaten - out copper, which form the arms, is a new and effective departure.

WROUGHT IRON.

I do not know any craft in which it is truer to say that the method of work suggests the design than in wrought iron.   Heat a bar or rod of iron to redness, and it can be easily bent and twisted into beautiful spirals and scrolls. Beat out the end, and the form of a leaf or flower can be given to it.   The leaves growing around an oriental poppy stem suggest a *motif* which has been used with various modifications in wrought iron through three centuries.   This can be seen by reference to Fig. 2 in Chapter I.

Iron itself suggests a certain severity of treatment which we find in the best work.   It can be elegant in construction and graceful and delicate in its details, but the whole work should hint at strength, for iron suggests strength, and therefore in the details I think it is a mistake to encrust the work with very delicately beaten-out forms suggesting paper festoons.   The backbone of the design should be the twisted rods and bars, and the utmost effect should be obtained by this simple twisting and hammering.

The supports of old inn signs made by the village smith, which still may be seen in country places, simple as they are, are on quite the right lines, for the smith twisted his iron while it was hot, making it take forms which could be most

easily produced : it was design springing out of craftsmanship, than which nothing can be more appropriate. The
basis of wrought-iron designs would seem to be the opp si-

Fig. 38.— Wrought Iron Stair Railing.   Hardman, Powell & Co.

tion of curves to straight lines, for the straight bar is
inseparable to wrought iron work besides affording a capital
foil to the curves and scrolls.

The gradual tapering of the end of a rod, or the splitting of it into two, three, or more smaller rods, suggests the form the design should take.   There is a tendency to be guarded against of making the details too naturalistic; imitating roses, for instance, seems to be overstepping the modesty of nature : it certainly is putting beaten iron to a false use, beside a simpler treatment is more effective. If the design springs out of the craftsmanship we should have less of this imitation.   A detail which takes an immense trouble to make is invariably on the wrong lines.   Carving cherry stones may display skill and ingenuity, but it does not atone for the grievously misdirected energy which makes the judicious grieve.

Many of the wrought-iron balustrades of the last century are excellent specimens of craftsmanship, for, being under cover, a more delicate and fanciful treatment was permissible than would be the case were the work exposed to the elements.   The skill of the smith is seen in the beaten-out leaves enwrapping the main lines of the design, and also in the beauty of the curves.   The appreciation of the subtleties of a curve shown in the 17th and 18th century iron-work tells one that the men who wrought them were artists.

An amateur taking up wrought iron should get a good blacksmith to instruct him in the methods of hammering, twisting and shaping iron while hot.   His instruction will probably end there, for unfortunately country blacksmiths have for so long not been asked to do anything needing a sense of beauty, that they would require instruction in the possibilities of their craft before they could do anything themselves.

The two Italian tripods, Figs. 39 and 41, are in the Birmingham Museum, where other good specimens of wrought iron may be seen. and at South Kensington Museum is an excellent collection of many periods and peoples.

The elaborate old hinges on church doors are excellent instances of what can be done with simple means. for nothing elaborate in workmanship is attempted. the whole effect being the result of curved lines.

The 17th century sword-rests in many of the City churches are beautiful specimens of workmanship. I give illustrations of two which I drew some time since for an article in *The Art Journal*. on " Art in the City Churches." Fig. 42.

I extract the following from an article on "Decoratively Wrought Iron," by J. M. O'Fallon, which appeared in the same paper.

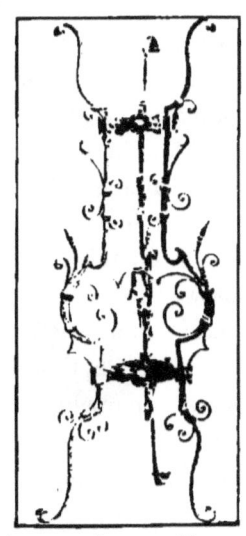

Fig. 39. Tripod, Wrought Iron, Italian, 1600.

"At the present hour charcoal iron is much preferred for these purposes. Great quantities of it come from Sweden in huge lumps called 'blooms.' which are afterwards reduced. rolled into sheets of varying thicknesses, or drawn out into different-sized rods. round or square-shaped. The sheets are selected for cutting or splitting up and working into all kinds of things, besides certain makes of leaves. petals. and imitations of similar natural growths. The rods in the process of smithing are thinned as wanted for stems. tendrils. and other parts of patterns; or they may be beaten out into

leaves; or, when desired, thickened up at the ends, shaped
into buds, and in many ways made into more or less tasteful
adjuncts of ornamental iron-work.

" We now enter more fully into our subject. The structural arrangement of a design being decided upon and
built up in the bar iron (this is occasionally *swaged* in part
—that is, beaten and shaped while hot betwixt two moulds
or swages), the ironsmith turns his attention to making the
ornamental filling for it; which may be a gate, a spandril,
or other heavy object, or a light object. Minor panellings
can seldom be welded into the principal framing, so, as a
rule, are attached by collars, screws, or rivets; even scroll-
work and leaves and husks may be so attached, but not
generally by the true craftsman—when you find him and he
is allowed to have his way. The principle that may be said
to actuate him when circumstances favour his carrying out
his own conceptions to completion, is that at least the
properly ornamental part of his work shall be founded on
natural forms, as in the best Gothic and Renaissance.
Unfortunately, the present competitive system under which
labour is conducted, and the consequent subdivision of
labour, has the workman its slave ; and ironsmithing, like
other originally ennobling handicrafts, is carried on in
separate departments. Forging and welding, even of leaves
and flowers, in most shops now form a distinct trade from
that of the beating out to a finish of the leaves or flowers ;
and both are occasionally the mere work of the stamper or
of the girl at the press. With stamping or pressed work
we do not concern ourselves now, but proceed to give a
short description of how a leaf is made from forging to
finish. This will, we hope, help the uninitiated to a fair

Fig. 40. Groups of Objects in Wrought Iron. By Edwin Fletcher.

Good examples of art applied to our everyday surroundings. See also Fig. 32, which shows that art is beginning to permeate life.

comprehension of the ins and outs of an ordinary specimen
of ornament of wrought iron in which such leaf is likely to
be present.   The smith gives it something of a rudimentary
shape, usually leaving the stem attached in the rough.   The
stem may be primary or secondary : as a rule it is secondary
for reducing in length or thickness, and welding on to the
primary, according to the run of the pattern.   The beating
towards finish is done at the
vice.   The rough forging is
held in the left hand on a
punch-shaped piece of steel,
V-grooved at the top, which
appears just over the grip of
the vice ; in the right hand a
hammer—elongated from the
'pene,' or striking end, to
what in an ordinary hammer
would be called the face, but
which is in reality another
pene—with the proper 'hang'
is brought down unerringly
on the rough, which is moved
along a little with each
stroke until the centre vein has
traversed its length.   During

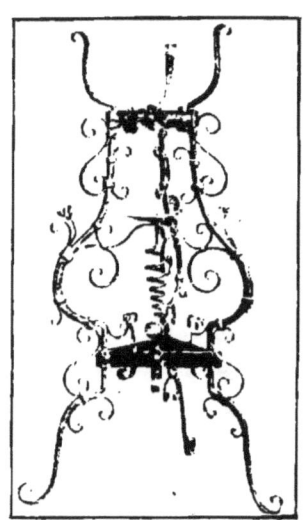

Fig. 41.—Tripod, Wrought Iron
Spiral   and   Scroll   Work.
Italian, 1600.

this operation the leaf is kept from sinking too much in the
middle by an occasional hit on either side of the vein.
The shorter veins, usually simple, but at times reticulate,
are produced with a lighter touch ; and the margins may be
left entire or variously cut or divided.   The leaf is bent in
several ways in imitation of nature, and according to the

SWORD RESTS

The crown and lion formed the
terminal, but owing to height of
cut had to be placed at side.

Fig. 12.

position it has to take in the work as a whole. The petals of flowers seldom require veining, but are bent about much after the same fashion as leaves. For assisting flower forms a ball-ended hammer is used on the thin iron, cut to size wanted, and, while being struck into shape, held over a hollowed-out or tubular form fixed in the vice. Stamens and pistils are added to flowers – when their presence is thought necessary, and the price allows. The chisel or chasing tool and hammer were often in the hands of the Mediæval and Renaissance worker in iron. He sculptured or beat up the cold metal into quaint figures and beautiful floriations and foliations without apparent effort, but with all the pleasure begotten of real love for his work. It is true that he sometimes—as in England so far back as the early part of the thirteenth century, and in the Ile de France, so famous for its blacksmithing, of which Notre-Dame has so many grand examples—assisted his work, generally while hot, with forms of dies and swages; but aids of this kind may be quite justifiable when governed by correct taste and discrimination such as were natural to the old ironsmiths; particularly while seeking to express details of special parts of patterns, and in their diapers and repeats. Love of Art for Art's sake was equivalent in those days to love of work for work's sake. The workman's attention was not absorbed in creating quantity before quality; nor the master, who was the best artificer, in calculating money profit before everything."

CHAPTER IV

JEWELLERY.

Fig. 43. Pendant in Gold and Enamel, with Pearl. By Alex. Fisher.

HERE we have an art which exists entirely for its beauty, and yet how wanting in daintiness and thought is the bulk of the jewellery we see staring at us in the shop windows! A jewel, I take it, should be unique, for to give such a thing to a friend is a compliment. Why not, therefore, have it made expressly for the recipient, as our verbal compliments are (or should be), and not some stock article possessed by any one who will put down so much money for it? To search out some artist working in the precious metals, and give him a commission to fashion some article expressly for the occasion, would seem to me to be a valued privilege, and one I am disposed to covet. No need to fear that the work would be repeated, for an artist hates doing again what he has once well done; when the work is finished it is put aside, for there are so many other ideas waiting to find a local habitation and a name.

A jewel, therefore, should always be unique. It is an

idea, having special reference to the person for whom it is, made definite in metal and helped it may be with gems; or if the gem itself is of great beauty, then the metal-work

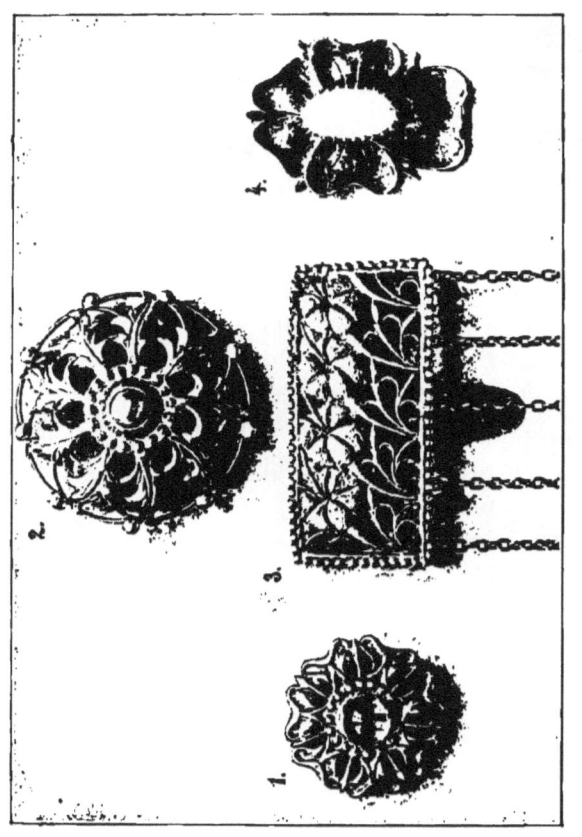

Fig. 44.—Modern Ornaments designed by Mr. C. R. Ashbee, architect, and executed by the Guild of Handicraft.

No. 1. Silver Brooch set with pale amethyst.
No. 2. Gold Brooch set with pearls, the property of Miss Ashbee.
No. 3. Silver Chatelaine.
(The above are cast after the original wax models.)
No. 4. Silver Brooch, hand-wrought, and set with a pearl.

must do all it can to lead up to the " precious " stone. The metal then becomes a beautiful framework to the gem.

To get out of the mechanical groove into which jewellery

has run for so long is the first necessity, and leads up to the
second one, originality. As one stands looking at the
glitter of a jeweller's shop, how one longs for an original
touch, a personal note, the expression of a mind instead of

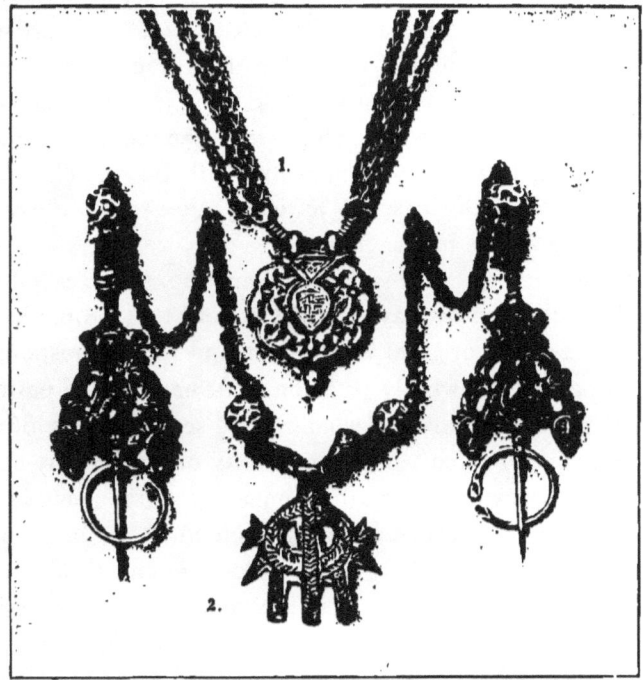

Fig. 45.

No. 1. Buddhist Ornament, the pendant on thin brass in relief.
No. 2. Kaby Ornament Clasp   white metal   with rough coral.

the output of machines. I am happy to say that in the
Royal Academy this last few years some few specimens of
jewellery have been shown. Mr. Alfred Gilbert, R.A., has
devoted much of his time to working in the precious metals
and his "Mayor of Preston's Chain" is one of the most

beautiful pieces of jewellery produced this century. This fact alone shows how the old lines of demarcation, which separated what used to be called *fine* art from the crafts, are effaced. Mr. Alex. Fisher and Mr. George Frampton have both exhibited beautiful specimens of fine metal-work, full of fancy and originality—invested *indeed* with artistic merit. A jeweller should remember that thoughtful human labour is, after all, the most valuable thing in the world, and therefore if, as I have elsewhere said, the value of metal-work should be in the workmanship, with how much more force is this in the case of jewellery, the *raison d'être* of whose existence is its beauty?

At the Arts and Crafts Exhibitions, too, some excellent jewellery has been displayed, and I believe that people have only to be shown original work to demand it. The responsibility does not rest wholly with the craftsman, for the patron should be on the look out whenever he sees the work of an original spirit, so that when opportunity occurs he may help the worker by extending his discriminating patronage to him; but an artist, whatever be the medium in which he works, must compel patronage by the force of his genius; he must do something so excellent that the onlooker cannot resist the appeal all good work makes, viz., to desire it, and if necessary go without something else to possess it. More is expected of the artist than of the public, for the former leads while the latter follows. A good many of us are waiting to have our fancy stirred by the work which is of good report, and therefore the craftsman must not wait until the public moves; he must not only direct the movement, but initiate it.

The revival of enamelling has encouraged artists to

make jewellery as an amusement if not professionally. I
am able to give a specimen of the work of Mr. George

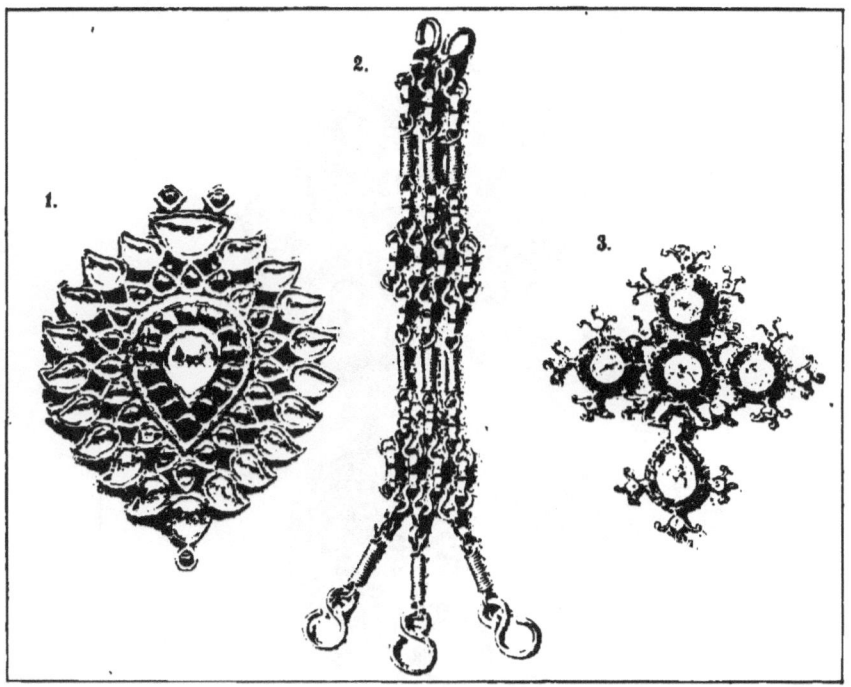

Fig. 46.

No. 1. Antique Indian Pendant, gold, set with jewels. From Messrs. Procter & Co.
No. 2. English Eighteenth-century Chain of gilt metal in triple series of links.
No. 3. Pendant, set with five large and many small crystals. French work from
Lower Normandy. Seventeenth century.
The two last from the South Kensington Museum.

Frampton in this direction,* but as it depends for its effect
upon the enamelling, only a bare idea of the jewel itself
can be obtained from the illustration. The pendant by

* The illustration will be found in the chapter on Enamelling.

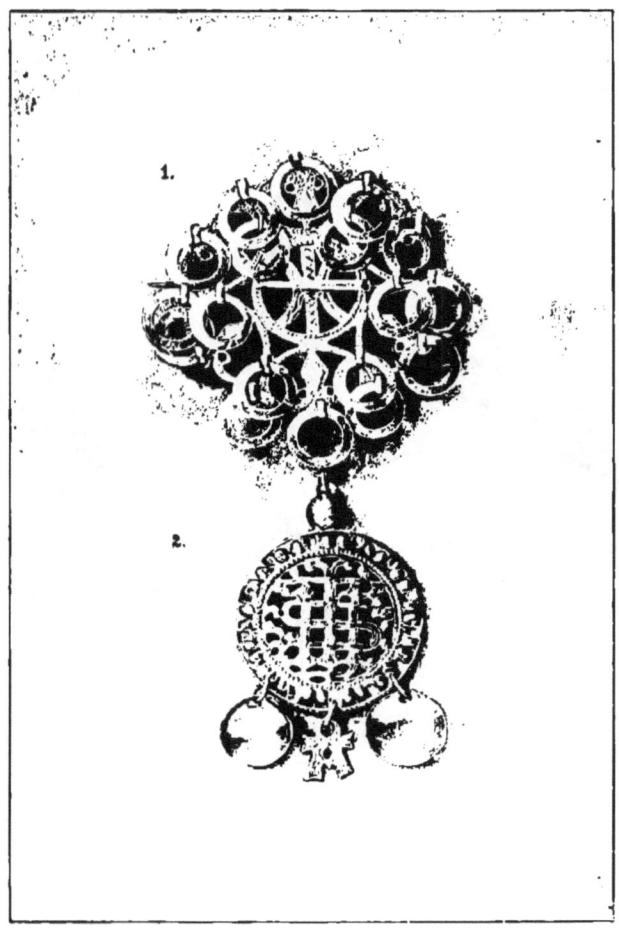

Fig. 47.

No. 1. Silver Brooch, Norwegian.
No. 2. Neck Ornament of silver-gilt, seventeenth century, Swedish.
    From the Torna district, in the province of Skåne.
      (Both in the South Kensington Museum.)

Mr. Fisher is a skilful piece of scroll weaving, and is reminiscent of Holbein's work in this direction. One of

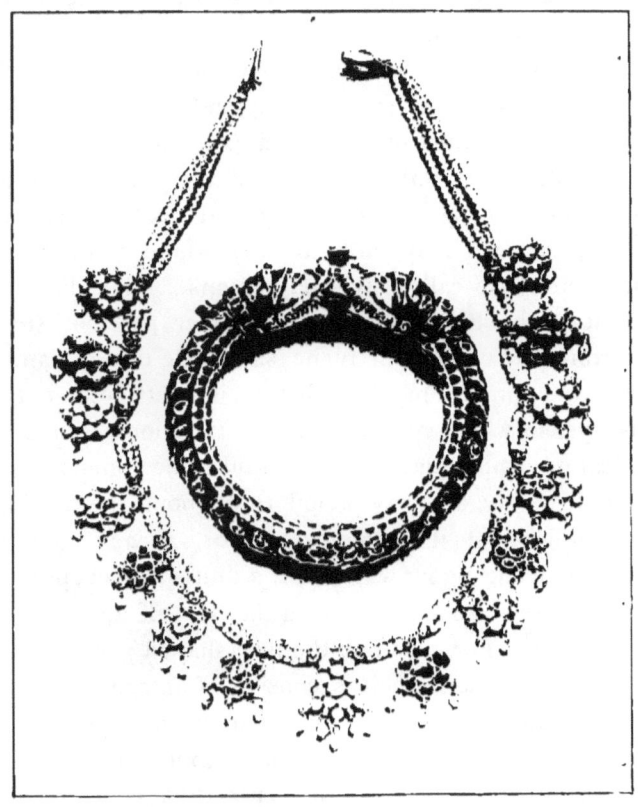

Fig. 18.

Necklace of Pearls, Pale Coral, and Precious Stones.
Good Example, decorated with coloured enamels and stones.
In South Kensington Museum.

its chief merits to me is that it gets away a long way away from trade jewellery.

I extract the following from an article contributed to *I*

Art Journal by Aymer Vallance, on Jewellery, some of the illustrations to which are also given, as they point out better than words how utterly worthless as art is the "jewellery" of the day.

"During the eighteenth century, in the ornaments of the wealthier classes, the stone-cutter and stone-setter had practically supplanted the artist in precious metals; and, from that date, it is only in such peasant jewellery as has been unaffected by ever-changing and ever-deteriorating fashions, that we may look for any sound traditions of design among so-called civilised nations. The misplaced ingenuity with which diamonds and other precious stones are tortured by us into the inane similitude of a garland of flowers or a spray of maidenhair fern, is in striking contrast to the system which governs the best traditional ornament. One feature, which may almost be said to be common to all artistic jewellery of every period throughout the world, is the simplicity of its ground-plan, or, at any rate, the uncompromising rigour with which a unit—in itself, perhaps, not so severe—is chosen to form the sum of an ornament by repetition. For example, the pear-shaped pendant (Fig. 46, No. 1), handsome as it is, consists of an aggregate of its own form on a reduced scale. The pear-shape and the triangle are, it will be seen without much difficulty, the elements on which the two ornaments (Fig. 45, Nos. 1 and 2 are based. The Norwegian and Swedish ornaments (Fig. 47, Nos. 1 and 2, both circular in plan, are further adorned with circular pendants, in the one case rings, and in the other concave discs. To the last is added a device frequently to be met with in Swedish jewellery. It is conjectured to be the monogram of the name Maria, or the initials of the angelic salutation, *Ave Maria.* Pendant drops, whether globules, discs, rings, lozenges, triangles, crescents, pear or pine shapes, are extensively used in ancient and traditional jewellery of many countries, and might, with advantage, be adopted by ourselves. Being attached in such a way as to be stirred with the wearer's every movement, the scintillations of the play of light upon them has won for them among the Easterns a name which means, in Arabic, lightning. Even where the impression conveyed is that of sumptuousness, it will generally be found on analysis that the unit is comparatively simple, as in the Indian necklace (Fig. 48 . This class of chain, consisting of separate plates linked or hinged together, was known in the England of Elizabeth as a carcanet. In certain parts of France peasant jewellery is still, or was until recently, made of

Fig. 49. -- Brooch with pale Amethyst set in Silver. (Full size.)

considerable artistic merit, after the manner of the old cross Fig. 46, No. 3 . It will be observed that the lower limb is hinged, a practical convenience which renders it less liable to get bent or snapped off in wear. Of the same period is the fob chain Fig. 46, No. 2 . It is both workmanlike in execution and admirable for its purpose."

I agree with the writer that some of the most beautiful jewellery is the aggregation of many simple units. The necklaces found by Schliemann at Troy are made on this

plan of linking a number of small pendants on to a chain
or chains, so that when on the neck it sways with every
movement.

At South Kensington Museum may be seen some peasant
jewellery from various parts of the Continent. It is both
artistic and effective and extraordinarily cheap, for the prices
given are attached to the labels. The necklace, in Fig. 48,

Fig. 50.—Carbuncle Brooch in Silver.   Full size.)

is built up of two simple units repeated a given number of
times, and yet how entirely admirable it is!

ON THE SETTING OF STONES.

To crowd a number of more or less valuable stones
together into a small space appears to be the ideal of the
jeweller, instead of making each gem an accent, a spot of

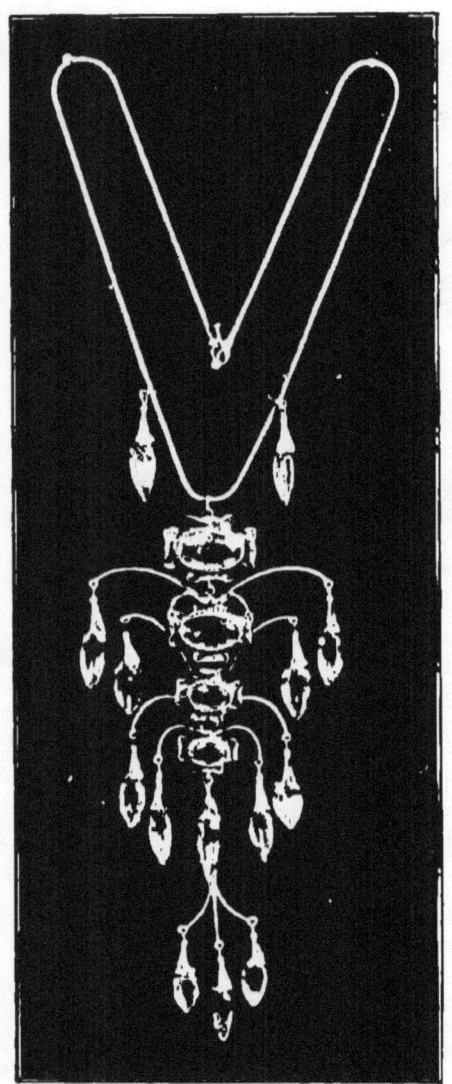

Fig. 31.   Pendant Topaz and Gold Necklace.   Reduced size.

brilliance or colour in the whole scheme. The setting should lead up to the gem, the one helping the other, and in the work of the sixteenth century it was so. Holbein designed some most beautiful jewellery. in which a perfect balance is preserved between the metal-work and the gems. I cannot do better in this connection than extract the following from an article by Mr. Ashbee on the setting of stones, with some of the illustrations from specimens of work executed under his supervision.

Fig. 52. — Treatment of Small Grey Pearl in hammered Silver. (Full size.)

Mr. C. R. Ashbee, I may remind my readers, has started, in an old Georgian house in Mile End Road, known as Essex House, a Guild of Handicraft, which has developed out of classes he inaugurated while residing at Toynbee Hall. Essex House is a regular workshop, as whatever is of use in a house is made, from a coal box to a necklace.

"In considering the question as to what one is to do in the setting of stones, I think the safest rule to be observed is that one must not bother much about their setting. The treatment of stones in metals should be a matter of feeling, of personal taste, of character. Apart from the technical, and I think less important, question as to whether a stone

should be set in a band turned over ⌇⌇⌇ or in a beaded

rim ⌇⌇ , a clip ⌇⌇ or a branched cusping

, there are a number of matters, more important really, which resolve themselves into artistic predilection. That rose topaz goes well with gold, especially grey gold ; that a carbuncle should be polished *en cabochon* and foiled, not faceted and set *à jour ;* that amethyst looks vulgar with gold, more particularly coloured gold ; that rubies should not

Fig. 53.—Set Sapphire and Moonstones with Grey Blue Enamel, set in Silver Wire. (The property of Mr. R. Ratcliffe Whitehead.)

be placed by themselves—these and a number of other matters in the setting of stones are not to be reasoned about. Circumstances may come in which they may be reversed ; all one can do is to shrug one's shoulders and say—so at least think I. Jewellery is a personal art in more ways than one.

" In the accompanying plates—which of course can give no idea of what is the most important thing of all, *viz.* so

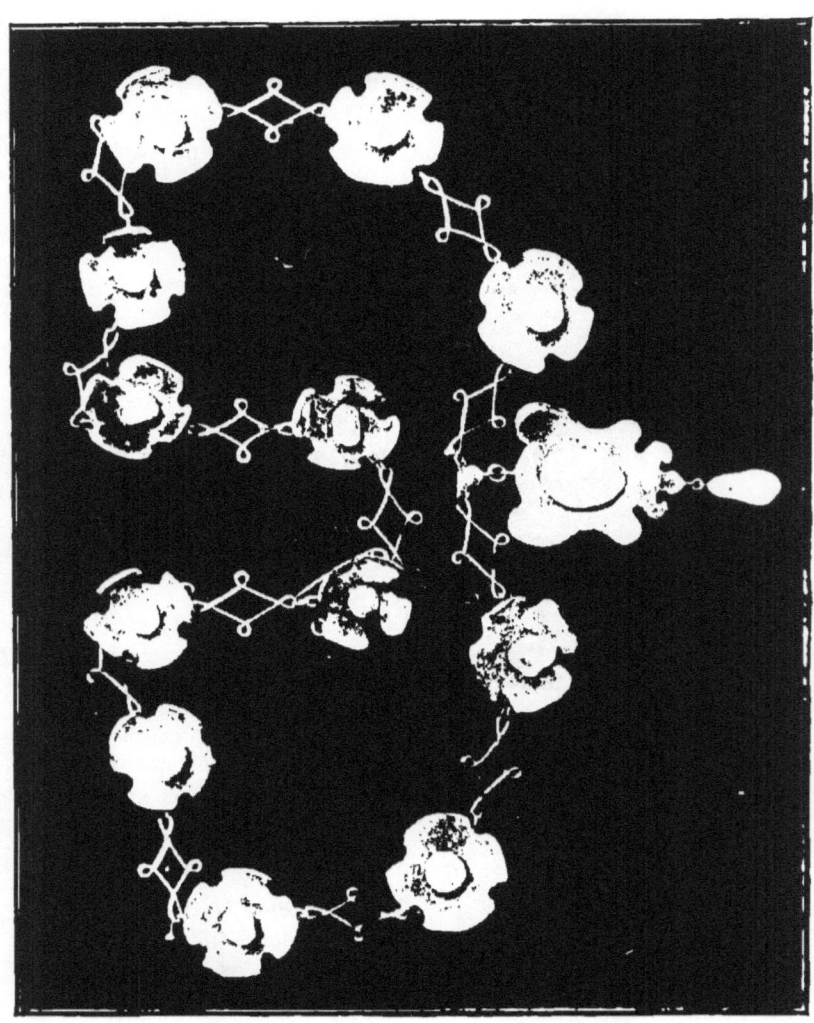

Fig. 54.— Necklace of Gold, with Blue Enamel, set with varying Grey Pearls.   (Half full size.)

I give some experiments of work executed from my designs at Essex House, in these different treatments.

"As to the arrangement of your setting, you should have your stone or group of stones before you and plan it out. I like to work in one of three ways—either with the pencil, painting curves in plan, section, and elevation, on a piece of paper till I feel the lines I want, the main curves and the big central stone shot forward into prominence; or with a piece of wire shaping curves that flow from one plane into another, and object to paper renderings; or with a piece of wax that will let itself be lovably pinched and petted, and holds the stones affectionately as you develop your work."

A great deal can be done with beaten silver, especially if enamelling comes into play. Simple beaten discs of silver attached to a chain by means of links, and enamelled, would give a most brilliant and varied effect. The jewel by Mr. George Frampton, given in the next chapter, Fig. 56, is an instance of an excellent and original result obtained by very simple means and no great expenditure of labour. The necklace (Fig. 54) is another instance of how excellent an effect can be obtained by comparatively simple means, if only the labour is directed by taste and originality.

CHAPTER V.

ENAMELLING ON METAL.

 GREAT revival has taken place in this very beautiful art within recent years, and work equal technically to any executed in the sixteenth century is being wrought now, while a much more varied palette is successfully employed by artists like Mr. Fisher. Why such an art should have been allowed to drop into desuetude is not understandable, for as a help to metal-work it at least was worth practising. The goldsmiths' work of Cellini and his time was greatly helped by being accented with enamels, while we have only to see the collection at South Kensington Museum, or the recent historical one at the Burlington Fine Arts Club, to realise what enamelling can do when in the hands of a master.

Mr. Alex. Fisher is one of the foremost enamellers of the day, as his work in the last two Academy exhibitions attests, and I am indebted to him for much information embodied in this article. The illustrations of enamels can never suggest the originals, for enamelling is essentially a *colour* art. That is, like stained glass, colour is its *raison d'être*, and nothing must be done that will check the display of this quality; even design itself must be sacrificed if

necessary. There must be no attempt at picture or miniature painting if it be at a loss of colour, for the enameller
must work to display the gem-like quality of his art. Mr.
Frampton, who does a little enamelling (two specimens of
his work are given, Figs. 56 and 57 , holds that to attempt
too much in the way of figure modelling is not to do the best
with the art. He himself goes in for a highly decorative
mosaic treatment, as the lid of the casket executed for the
Skinners' Company shows. The human figure plays a large
part in Mr. Fisher's designs, and he shows skill as a draughtsman and power of decorative composition with no loss of
the colour quality. The jewel by Mr. Frampton has only
so much design as gives excuse for a display of gem like
colour, and certainly so beautiful is the effect of translucent
enamels on silver that I can well understand the disposition
to make the work a mere palette of gems, so to say.

Copper and silver are the metals most usually enamelled.
In a large work copper would be used, and gold or silver
would be introduced as thin plates of metal soldered to the
copper and then enamelled over. By this introduction of
gold and silver under transparent enamel the most brilliant
and varied effects can be obtained. A ruby enamel would
have three different tones as it came upon copper, silver,
and gold.

The enamels are of two parts—the colouring matter,
usually a metallic oxide, and a flux or fusible material which
requires heat to melt it and so fix it to the metal. The
enamels in their raw state are like lumps of dull-coloured
glass, and require to be pounded in a mortar or ground on
a slab with a glass muller until they are a coarse
powder, and they are then mixed with water and painted

on the metal more or less thickly. The colour only comes out in the firing, for a ruby may look amber, and blue a dull yellow before firing, so a good deal of judgment is required to know what you are doing. In this respect it is like underglaze pottery painting, for there the colours undergo great changes in the kiln.

Fig. 55.—Repoussé Steel and Enamelled Casket. By Alex. Fisher.

The enamels are fired in a small muffle heated with gas, and is the work of only a few minutes, but an elaborate enamel, such as the figure on Mr. Fisher's casket, is the result of painting one enamel over another, and is therefore fired many times. Great care and knowledge is here required to realise the ultimate effect of one colour over another, and to see that the enamels are put to the right heat, for too much heat would irretrievably ruin the whole work.

Then, again, some enamels are transparent, others opaque, and much of the effect is obtained by the opaque enamels playing into the transparent ones. Sometimes an enamel will have transparent colours in the background, while the design is opaque. This is the case in many of the old Limoges pieces where the figures are in white on a deep blue ground. To obtain definition colours similar to those used in china painting are employed and in much the same way. As some enamels fuse at a lower temperature than others, these have to be put on last. It does not appear to be a difficult art at the outset, to one accustomed to underglaze pottery painting, but to carry it to perfection needs a long apprenticeship. Mr. Fisher was an enameller on pottery before he took up metal-work, and it was while holding a scholarship at South Kensington that he learned metal enamelling of a M. Dalpayrat, a French enameller, who gave a series of demonstrations at Mr. Armstrong's initiative at the schools. "I resolved," he told me, "from the outset to master the whole subject, and commenced to experiment on the making of enamels, so that I might understand completely their capabilities and how best to develop them. This was an arduous undertaking, being more the work of a chemist than an artist; but I now make all my best colours, though where I can buy any that are of any use to me I do."

Enamels were added to gold and silversmiths' work from the fourth to the seventh century. It became of the greatest importance in Byzantine goldsmiths' work, when Christianity became the religion of the State, and has been used by them continually down to our own time. An enameller is of necessity a worker in metal.

We will now briefly glance at the various processes employed by enamellers.

Champlevé.—This is the simplest, and probably the oldest, form. It consists in cutting out spaces on a thickish plate

Fig. 56. — Enamelled Silver Jewel. By Geo. Frampton, A.R.A.

of metal, and filling these in with powdered enamel. It is then fired and afterwards filed down even with the metal and then polished. The few specimens of Saxon work, such as King Alfred's jewel, are enriched in this way.

[*Niello* is the name given to a black composition made of silver, lead, sulphur, and copper, which is laid, in the form of powder, in lines or cavities prepared for it on a surface of silver. It is then passed through the furnace, when it is melted and becomes incorporated with the metal. It is mentioned as early as the beginning of the ninth century.]

Cloisonné is a similar process, except that the spaces are made by wire of gold, silver, or hard brass soldered on to the metal, usually copper.

These "enclosures" are filled with enamels applied in the form of a paste. The work is then fired and the surface given to it by rubbing the enamels over with stones until the whole surface is smooth. The best specimens are hand polished, and should have a soft, precious surface like some beautiful fruit. Japanese enamels almost entirely consist of this kind, and they are, without doubt, the greatest masters of this branch of the art, and the skill with which a Japanese solders down the filigree bands to form the enclosures (and the design) must be seen to be appreciated. Japanese Cloisonné is generally opaque.

Bassitaille.—The space to be enamelled is beaten or cut below the surface of the metal and then carved or beaten in low relief, so that when the transparent enamel is placed over this the modelling is seen through it, giving an extremely beautiful brilliancy to the enamel, and at the same time a very fine sense of form to the modelling. This enamel had its origin in Italy about the thirteenth century, and some of the most beautiful pieces of goldsmiths' work have parts or points coloured by this method. It was carried to perfection by Cellini and his pupils and contemporaries. One of the finest examples of this method is seen in the cup at the British Museum known as the St. Agnes cup, the enamel being of great splendour on fine gold.

Plique à Jour.—The pattern is just made in gold or silver wire soldered together, much in the same way as the lead in stained glass, but unlike the glass the enamel is fused

Fig. 57.—Inside of Lid of Casket, showing enamel. By Geo. Frampton, A.R.A.

into these spaces without a ground. This work is extremely delicate and fairy-like, and seemed to Mr. Fisher at one time to present an insuperable difficulty, but he at length overcame it.

Limoges generally consists in a subject being painted in a semi-opaque white enamel, on a dark ground in which the thickness and degrees of thinness of the white give the light and shade. This is sometimes coloured with transparent enamel. The well-known Battersea enamels of the eighteenth century, many examples of which are to be seen in South Kensington Museum, were done by first covering the metal with opaque white enamel, and then firing it and painting on the vitrified surface in ordinary china colours.

The qualities which appeal to one most in enamelling of a transparent kind (that is, where the metal ground is distinctly seen through the enamel) are brilliancy and preciousness. This latter quality is almost entirely over-looked, and yet to my mind it is the most exquisite of all. It is almost always found in early work, which is partly due to the love, the reverence, and the humanity of the ancient craftsmen. I mean by this the distinctly human effort as contrasted with the machine work of to-day. The Celtic and Byzantine enamels have all the perfection one can possibly desire in this respect. Mr. Fisher might have used the words of Rabbi Ben Ezra : not " on the vulgar mass called ' work ' must sentence pass, things done, that took the eye and had the price ; " but that work the outcome of the desire to express all that is in one which " the world's coarse thumb and finger failed to plumb."

The historical exhibition of enamels at the Burlington Fine Arts Club, in the summer of 1897, showed what has been done in the past. The sixteenth century enamels are probably some of the finest ever wrought until our own time. The subjects were often taken from prints after pictures by Raphael and his contemporaries, and the cuts and engravings of Dürer. The old enamellers were very fond of effects *en grisaille*, and a large number of pieces made at Limoges are of a dark purplish black or blue, with the design in white slightly tinted.

Enamelling, like all vitrified processes, is permanent, and there can be no question as to its suitability as a decoration to metal. For plaques, for furniture too, the most brilliant effects can be obtained which, when set in dark wood, would be particularly handsome as decoration. A realistic treatment is not the idea to go for, but a decorative or ornamental treatment of plant, animal or human form. The copying of pictures is a mistake, as the artist is cramped all the time by the necessity of observing his design, and the quality of his enamel will suffer in consequence. If he, on the other hand, carry out his own design, he has no restrictions of that kind, and can therefore develop his art to its utmost capacity.

Mr. Fisher teaches enamelling at the School of Arts and Crafts established by the County Council in Regent Street, and also at the Technical School, Finsbury, and from work he showed me executed by pupils at the latter place I should say there is a great future before enamelling. A very simple class of design is very effective, and great value is given to the design by the method of reproduction.

CHAPTER VI.

POTTERS AND PAINTERS.

"Time's wheel runs back or stops: Potter and clay endure."
Rabbi Ben Ezra.

THE life's story of most eminent potters is one of unending struggle against disheartening difficulties only partially conquered by persistent hopefulness and patience. William De Morgan, who may be taken as London's representative potter, has shared, with men like Palissy, many of the trials which make the old French potter's life so stimulating to those struggling towards success; for if De Morgan did not have to use the household furniture wherewith to kindle his kiln, he, in his early experiments, set fire to the house in Fitzroy Square, where he had fixed up a small muffle. That is now twenty-five years ago, and all this while has our London potter been experimenting and searching for more excellent ways; and from what one knows of the man, he will continue in his pioneer course, for, like the artist-craftsman he is, there can be nothing finite in his work. De Morgan had taken those lines of Browning's to heart and acted upon them : —

> " So, take and use thy work,
> Amend what flaws may lurk,
> What strain i' the stuff, what warpings past the aim ! "

The end is never, but always something to be reached, for achievement is only a halting-place or coign of 'vantage from which to make fresh efforts. Alexander should have been a potter, and then he would not have said there were no more worlds for him to conquer.

Where Mr. De Morgan lives in a social sense does not concern us, for he is most "at home" at his pottery in Chelsea, and it was my privilege to be taken round the place by the master potter himself. Everything there had been thought out and constructed under De Morgan's own initiative, for, as he told me, he never accepted what came to his hand, but has had to reach everything for himself by experiment. Even when he stayed in the potteries years ago, expressly to acquire technique, he did not learn what he easily might have been taught through his desire to start *de novo*, and it is in this spirit he still works. At one time he imported tiles from Stourbridge, and would only paint them at his pottery, but as all the tiles in the potteries are made of compressed dust, they will not stand exposure to the varying temperatures without breaking, or the surface flaking off, and Mr. De Morgan said that this fact had done more to discourage the use of tiles in decoration than anything. Now he makes his own tiles from clay sent from Stourbridge mixed with ground firebrick and old seggars. These tiles stand the weather perfectly, as a specimen shown to me testified, which had been in a London window-box for eleven years.

The painting, too, instead of being done on the tile itself, is done on thin paper, and this is stuck down on the surface of slip which De Morgan always uses to cover the dark body. The glaze is then put over the paper, and in the

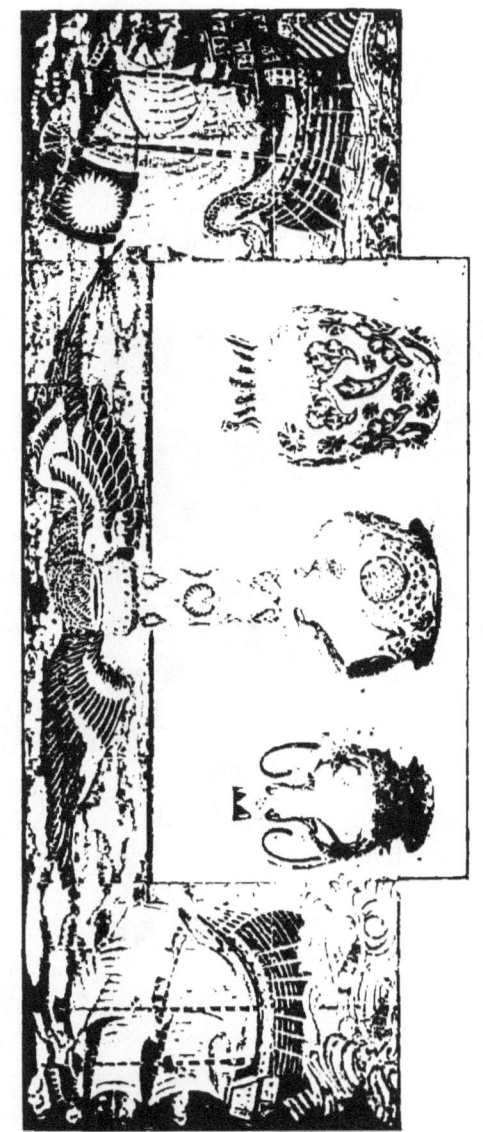

Fig. 58.   De Morgan Ware.

A Tile Panel for fire-place; three Vases thrown and decorated at the Chelsea Pottery.

firing this entirely disappears. De Morgan has no secrets. His experience, gained at so great a cost, is freely at the disposal of any potter. " Perhaps I know," he said to me, " more chemistry than many potters do, and more art than most chemists."

His pots are all finished on the wheel, for he does not believe in throwing them rough and then finishing them on the lathe, as is the usual practice. " It is a most deadly

Fig. 59.—De Morgan Ware.

occupation for the men, as the dust produced in lathing clay, which must be ' bone dry,' is most injurious to the lungs."

Mr. De Morgan hopes soon to make articles of household use, and he showed me some teapots in hand with a special kind of strainer contrived with much ingenuity. There are two large kilns and two smaller ones in use ; the largest is capable of holding some thirty thousand six-inch tiles.

I confess I write sympathetically about potters as I do about glass painters, for I was trained in both crafts in my youth, and at one time had a kiln of my own. De Morgan was led from painting glass to turn his attention to pottery, as I did. I mention this simply because, to realise a potter's difficulties, one needs an acquaintance with the craft. When one remembers that fire is a potter's necessary servant (and we know what a bad master it is), we at once realise that he has difficulties to encounter which do not beset the painter, who has not to submit his efforts when he has completed them to such a trying ordeal as a kiln, even if he have to submit his works to the hanging committee of an exhibition. It is an ignorant arrogance, therefore, which makes a quite mediocre painter of pictures look down upon a potter as of coarser clay than himself.

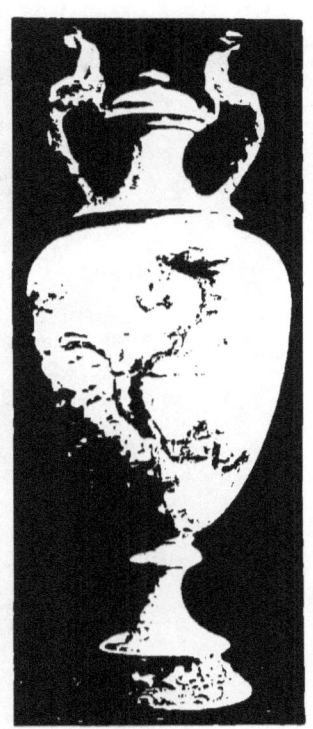

Fig. 60.—Lambeth Faience.

With the usual lack of patronage bestowed upon the unobtrusive worker, who cannot or will not advertise himself, and on the stimulus supplied by his desire to conquer, De Morgan has slowly overcome the technical difficulties which were before him, and produced work most excellent in its kind. And what are these difficulties? The body or clay used in the pottery, the colours, the glaze, and the firing; these are the several arcs of the circle, and the problem is to make them into the " perfect round."

Mr. De Morgan was invited by the Minister of Public

Instruction at Cairo to draw up a report on the " Feasibility of a Manufacture of Glazed Pottery in Egypt." He certainly turned to the country lying east of Egypt for inspiration, and took as his samplers the Persian pottery of the seventeenth and eighteenth centuries (also known as Damascus and Rhodian), which is noted for the richness of its glaze, giving the painted decoration (always under the glaze) a soft gem-like brilliance quite unsurpassed in pottery. The glaze, as every potter knows, is the most important consideration; and the thick coating

Fig. 61.—De Morgan Ware.

of glass De Morgan gives his pottery, mingling with the colours, produces a softness (the colours melting into the glaze softens the edges of the painting) and gem-like transparency which, as a practical pottery painter, I always envied.

Perhaps the most interesting work turned out at the Chelsea Pottery is the celebrated lustre ware. De Morgan's attention was first directed to lustre by noticing the iridescence seen on glass when the yellow stain, due to chloride of silver, is overfired. Copper and silver are the two metals used at Chelsea in the production of lustre, the former yielding a ruby, and the latter a yellow lustre. The Hispano-Mauresque ware is decorated in lustres, and the old sixteenth-century majolica is lustrous, but I doubt whether

Fig. 62.—De Morgan Tiles.

lustre of old times is superior to the best specimens produced by De Morgan. As a good deal of misconception exists as to what lustre is, I may state briefly that it is the result of reducing the metals which are painted upon the glazed surface (usually a tin glaze) mixed with some infusible earth, by charging the muffle when at a dull red heat with wood or other vegetable smoke. When cold, the material used with the metals is rubbed off, leaving the lustre beneath. The most exact conditions have to be

observed to produce good results, for too much heat and an
excess or lack of smoke will spoil the kiln. The excitement
attending the opening of a kiln must be lived through to
be realised; so also must the disappointment when nothing
but failure is encountered, and the painter's labour is thrown
away.

De Morgan, in the conclusion of a lecture on Lustre,
delivered before the Society of Arts, said: "I can only
say that if anyone sees his way to using the material to good
purpose, my experience, which I regard as an entirely
chemical and mechanical one, is quite at his disposal."

Fig. 63.—Amateur's Work.   By Thackery Turner.

Nevertheless, he is largely his own designer, and I shall
leave the specimens given in this article to speak for
themselves. The colour beauty, which is always the chief
charm of pottery, cannot be indicated in the illustrations.

Martin ware is another production of London. The
kilns are in Fulham, and it has been noted for its salt-
glazed ware for some years. The master-potter is one of
those unobtrusive, non-advertising craftsmen, content to
turn out excellent work year after year, trusting to the
patronage of the discriminating. The show-rooms used to
be (and I believe still are) in Brownlow Street, Holborn,

and those collecting modern pottery should examine Martin
ware, as it is excellent in its kind.

In dealing with a firm like Doulton's, the personality
which, in De Morgan's case, is so interesting, is wanting.
Doulton's is a big concern, a manufactory carried on on a
gigantic scale, and might, with-
out much stretch of metaphor,
be likened to a sponge, which,
seemingly one organism, consists in reality of a colony.
Originally founded in Vaux-
hall, in 1815, John Doulton
and J. Watts established themselves later at Lambeth, and
in 1846 the present head of
the firm, and son of the original
John Doulton, commenced
the manufacture of stoneware
drain-pipes and other sanitary
pottery, and it was not until
1866 that the opportunity was
taken to connect Art workmanship with the previous rough
productions. Within the last
twenty years the productions

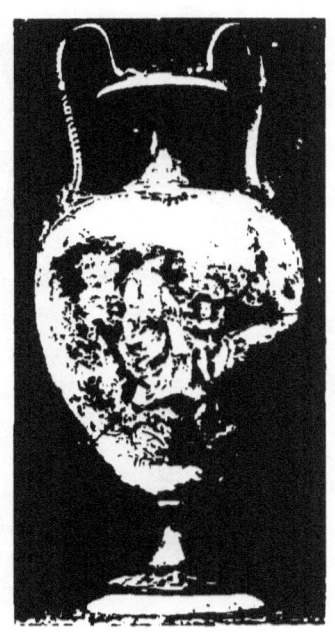

Fig. 64.—Lambeth Faience.

of Lambeth pottery have been prominently before the public.
It deserves to be stated here that the individual has not at
Lambeth become merely a sort of cog on the wheel of
the huge machine, for it has been the custom for Doulton's
craftsmen to sign the pieces they are severally responsible
for; and in this way the two Miss Barlows' spontaneous

sketches of animal and birds incised in the wet clay are
known to those familiar with modern pottery.

From what I saw during a visit to the pottery I take it
that a fair measure of liberty is allowed all those who rise

Fig. 65.—Solon Ware.   By Minton.

above the rank of mere "hands," so that, within certain
limits, they can give their art instincts proper expression.

This is as it should be, for it is only in this way that
uniqueness can be imparted to the productions of the
Lambeth pottery.   To feel that you have one of an infinite
number of similar vases detracts from the satisfaction of
possession, and the mechanical uniformity of manufacture

is avoided if each piece has some individuality attaching to
it.　Art cannot be manufactured, and the sooner that is
recognised the better.　Messrs. Doulton have of necessity
to cater for a general, and therefore perhaps an uncritical,
unresponsive, public ; but the more they seek to develope
originality in their craftsmen, so that each piece has a spontaneous flow of life and thought, the expression of some mood
or emotion about it, the higher will the productions of the Lambeth pottery rank.　Women have always been largely employed
at Doulton's, and it is work certainly well within the faculties
of women, for the manipulation of wet clay is one necessitating patience, finger dexterity and deftness—qualities
associated more with women than men.

The Lambeth kilns produce two classes of pottery —
stoneware, which is salt-glazed ; and painted ware, which is
glazed afterwards with a moderately soft glaze.　The former
is, I should say, that which will gain for Lambeth its distinction, as it was evolved naturally from the ruder drain-pipe.
The *process of salt glazing* is not applicable to any other
kind of ware than stoneware, as the glaze is really formed
by the partial fusion of the clay itself.　During the last stage
of firing, when the ware is just on the point of vitrifaction,
common salt is thrown into the kiln.　The decomposition of
the salt fills the kiln with dense fumes of salt vapour, producing on the wares a gloss or glaze of silicate of soda
exceedingly hard and thin, exactly even over all parts of the
surface and hiding not the least touch left by the etching or
modelling tool.　Salt-glazed ware is an ideal pottery, and
there is a charm about the surface and colour of salt-glazed
ware which is unlike any other.　"Doulton ware," as it is
termed, follows in style of decoration the Grès de Flandres

Fig. 66.—Joseph is Sold to the Midianites. Tinworth Modelled Terra-Cotta.

of the seventeenth century, modelled or applied decoration being its leading feature.

I have a feeling that the fault of a good deal of modern pottery is that it is over-decorated—a fault as bad as a woman being over-dressed. It lacks selection and restraint, and the piece is made an excuse for the employment of decorative *motifs*. The ware, which in itself is beautiful, or should be, is so broken up that a busy rococo effect, rather than dignity and repose, is the result, and the eye gains no satisfaction from the ware itself. As a painter would say, it lacks breadth.

Stoneware, being fired in an open kiln and to a very high temperature, is not adapted for much painting. Blue was the chief colour used in the Flemish ware, but the palette has been extended to include celadon and browns of different shades. These have

Fig. 67.—" Morning " Vase.
By Copeland.

to be painted on with fluxes, which fuse only at the high temperature the ware is put to.

The painted ware, or " Lambeth Faience," as it is termed, is decorated in the biscuit state, and afterwards glazed and fired. The temperature this ware is fired to is much lower than stoneware, and the articles are not exposed to the flames, but are protected in fire-clay boxes. The palette is much more varied, and the treatment of the decoration is therefore confined to the work of the brush and is chiefly floral, though some excellent figure work is produced. The colouring of this faïence, owing to the warm soft glaze, is very harmonious.

The modelled decoration of George Tinworth, John Broad, and others, is of very high character indeed, and evinces fine technical skill and artistic perception. Some of the terra-cotta figure work turned out for the decoration of buildings is very excellent. Sculptors would find it a most pleasant material to work in, and there is no reason why many of them should not turn their attention to architectural modelling.

Fig. 68.—Holbein Ware. By Doulton & Co., Burslem.

A pottery is certainly one of the most interesting hives of industry to visit, and few who have watched a "thrower" evolve from a lump of clay with his thumb and finger and revolving wheel a beautiful shape, have not wished to try their hand at such cunning work, in which high manipulative skill has to be accompanied by quickness of eye and a rare intuition.

A few years ago china-painting was the rage, and almost every young lady, whether she painted on any other material or not, thought she could decorate a china plate. The craze died out, and it is rare now to hear of an amateur

painting china. Mr. Thackery Turner told me that he took
up china painting in 1882, when he started in practice as an
architect, as an exercise in designing. He got a firm at
Burslem to supply him with bisque (unglazed china), and
when painted he got them to glaze and fire for him. Mr.
Turner at first tried French colours, but gave them up for
Staffordshire trade colours. I quite endorse what he says
about under-glaze painting having the quality of a wet pebble,

Fig. 69.—Design for Majolica Plaque.   By G. Roots.
(South Kensington.)

but while it was easy to get work painted in enamels on the
glaze fired in London, it was difficult without sending to the
potteries to get ware glazed and fired, and amateurs, therefore, wisely confined their chief attention to overglaze work.
Considering what strange crazes the world takes to, china-
painting cannot be said to have been the maddest. Indeed,
ten years ago some most excellent work was being done by
amateurs.

Speaking from some years of experience as a painter of

pottery, I can say that though there are many disappointments through work being spoilt in the kiln, yet there are moments of exaltation when some work comes out particularly successfully. For purely decorative effects, where colour enters largely into play, underglaze work is far before that painted on the glaze and fired in a muffle. Several potteries on a small scale have sprung up since I was a "'prentice han'," in which the "art" is very much *en*

Fig. 70.—Persian Painted Tile.
Doulton & Co.

évidence, and some of these efforts at getting individuality into the work will in time bear fruit. But a really fine school of craftsmanship takes long to build up anywhere and at any time, especially in this country, where to do everything by machinery, or some mechanical process, is the direction advance makes for. The painter of pottery must be the author of the design as well as the executant if the best results are to be reached. That division into "designers" and "painters" is fatal to the best results. The proprietors of potteries should keep their eyes upon their apprentices, and give those who evince talent every possible advantage to become artists in their crafts. There is much more discrimination abroad than there was fifteen years ago, and manufacturers will find it necessary, on the purely economic grounds of self-defence, "to invest their products with artistic merit " if they are to hold their position in the markets of the world.

Fig. 71.—Tile Panel. Columbines. By W. C. Dean. South Kensington.)

The majolica plaque by G. Roots, and the painted tile panel by W. C. Dean, were prize designs at South Kensington. The latter is skilfully contrived so that the square shape of the 6-in. tiles is ingeniously disguised by the pattern.

Fig. 72, again, is cleverly designed to get a feeling of big-ness, though the

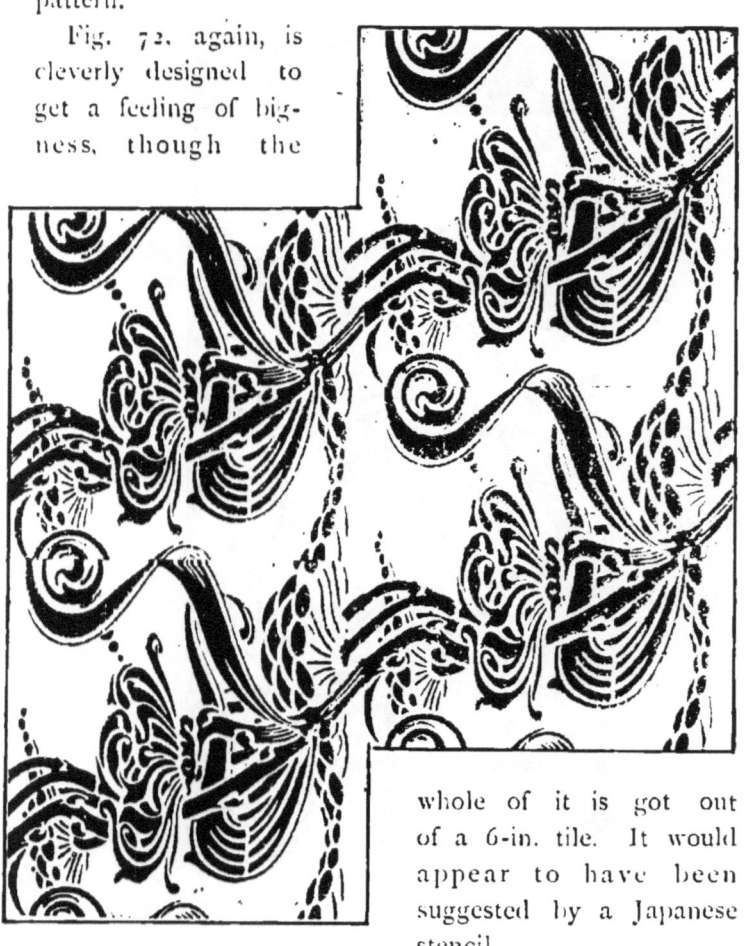

Fig. 72.—Painted Tiles.   Pilkington's.

whole of it is got out of a 6-in. tile. It would appear to have been suggested by a Japanese stencil.

One cannot end this chapter without reference to the work of the Staffordshire potteries, seeing that the bulk of

the ware in general use is made in that district. The illustrations of work by Minton, Copeland, and Doulton & Co.,
Burslem, must speak for themselves, but it is fair to say that
the charm of pottery, which is largely its colour, is in no
way suggested in the illustrations.

The *pâte-sur-pâte* work of Mr. Solon is perhaps the most
distinctive pottery of a purely artistic character turned out
there. The wonderful skill of this artist and the delicacy of
his drawing puts Mr. Solon's work far ahead of most other
decorated pottery. If I were to give a general criticism of
much of the Staffordshire art pottery it would be that a certain

Fig. 73.—Amateur's Work.   By Thackery Turner.

decorative fitness is wanting in it. A tendency towards a
highly pictorial treatment should, it seems to me, give place
to a more ornamental one. It is a colour art more than anything, and therefore the palette should be studied even before
drawing, *i.e.*, the potter should become acquainted with his
colours and what can be produced with them, what class of
effects to strive for, and how he can develop the resources
at his command. Surveying the craft generally, it is
apparent that pottery painting lacks distinction by its
want of originality in decorating the work of the potter's
wheel. An effort is being made in certain directions to
produce painted pottery of strong individuality and deco-

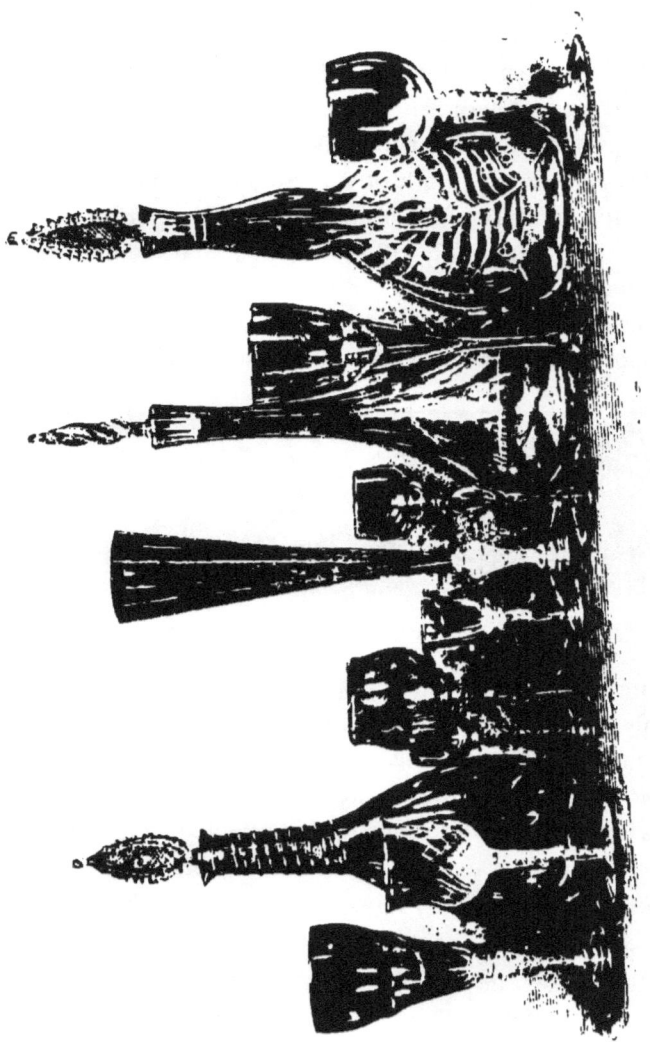

Fig. 74.—Whiteman Blown Glass.

rative fitness—to get away from the "factory," in fact; and we can only hope that these efforts will be crowned with success.

The plan in the potteries of taking lads as apprentices for seven years makes excellent workmen of those who are at all bent that way, but the art training is far too much neglected. What they learn in this way is what they pick up in the evening in the school of art, and after a long day in a factory the edge is much taken off for such routine tuition. What would be of much help and stimulus would be instruction by a skilled potter *who was an artist*, and the painting under his direction of original work. The life of the workmen is almost entirely ignored in factories, and from what I have heard from those who have passed through the "potteries," the factory system kills the art, which, like a delicate plant, withers away under this treatment. Then, too, one notices that under such a system craftsmanship always seems divorced from design, instead of the two developing simultaneously, the one helping the other. It shows into what a state our manufactories have fallen, that we have on the one hand a race of mechanics more or less skilful, but with no ideas, and on the other a few selected individuals who are specially engaged to direct this labour.

CHAPTER VII

GLASS PAINTERS.

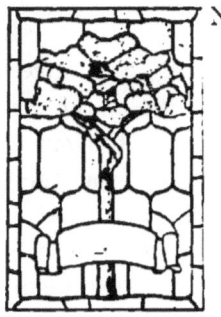

Fig. 75.
Small Window.
By C. Whall.

N these days of interviewing it is notable that Art craftsmen have not supplied much copy to that Autolycus of the moment, the journalist. Very mediocre painters of easel pictures, and illustrators with the slenderest cheap talent, have been interviewed, but with a few exceptions the workers engaged in the Art crafts, such as glass-painting, go on doing their work, and outside a small circle are little known because they are so rarely brought before the public gaze. Not that there would be anything gained by interviewing them, in a society sense, to discuss their favourite food and furniture, the decorations in their drawing-rooms, and their favourite pipes and pugs. But a peep at a few of the representative Art craftsmen, who are forming the impulses which will move those who come after, with a glance at their work, what are their aims, what their accomplishments, may help us the better to appreciate their efforts. It may also tend to make our praise discriminating, and so encourage the artist ; for nothing is so invigorating as intelligent appreciation, just as the applause of the ignorant is the most deadening stimulus he can receive.

My object, therefore, will be to discuss the recent productions of a few of the more representative men in this craft, at the same time giving, through the medium of illustrations, an idea of what is being done to give distinction to this Art of our day; so that we may not pass by what is worthy and of good report when we see it.

Modern glass-painting came into existence within the last half-century, largely through the efforts of a barrister, Charles Winston. This writer's book on the subject of old glass is a standard work, and should be consulted by those who wish to understand why the glass of the thirteenth to the fifteenth centuries is so much finer than anything which has been done till within our own day ;—for it is a mistake to assume that no modern glass equals the finest old work. With our increased knowledge of chemistry and our modern appliances, as well as our power of drawing, we ought to produce better work than was possible in the Middle Ages, and occasionally, it must be admitted, we do.

What are the chief qualities we look for in a painted window? First, colour. The most dazzling and unapproachable effects of colour are obtained by putting together pieces of coloured glass, for the material can, by the use of metallic oxides, be tinted to every rainbow hue. A window, therefore, might be likened to slices of large gems put together as a mosaic is, with bands of lead to hold the pieces together. We might simply lead a number of pieces of coloured glass together as a girl sews patchwork, and thus get a beautiful palette of colour.

I

Fig. 76.—Designed by the late J. D. Watson, for Messrs. Campbell, Smith, & Co.

Some painters tell us that a picture should be a wondrous palette of colour, and that design or idea should be quite subordinate. I think that such a statement holds truer of a window than a picture, for coloured glass can be, from its transparency, more beautiful than any pigments. Now let us look at the average windows we see in churches, and viewing them merely as colour see how they stand criticism. A large number of such windows are too heavy in key, too little white or tinted white glass being employed. This is bad in two ways, bad in itself and bad for the building, because such heavy windows prevent the proper amount of light entering, producing not a "dim religious light," but darkness, making nothing visible. An interesting church like St. Helen's, Bishopsgate, is spoilt by the heaviness of the windows. They are all coloured, so that on the ordinary days of the City very little is clearly discernible, and the beautiful and interesting tombs cannot be properly appreciated in such obscurity. The object of a window is to admit light—there can be no question about that; and though it is a great gain to a church to have the light modified and warmed by passing through tinted glass, with richer-coloured glass to give glow and accent, the primary object of a window must not be lost sight of, namely, to admit light.

Not only may a window be too dark from the excess of coloured glass in it, but also from the amount of paint upon the glass; as in the case of the celebrated windows which Reynolds designed for New College, Oxford. Here no coloured glass is used, but the effect of an oil painting is attempted, all brilliancy being lost in the mistaken effort, and the absence of the gem-like quality, specially acceptable in stained glass, is therefore painfully felt.

This brings us to the next consideration : the design of a window.   In church windows symbolism largely regulates the design, but that aspect of the question is outside my

Fig. 77.   Panels of Glass showing the effect obtained by use of Coloured Glass and Leads only.   By Messrs. Guthrie, of Glasgow.

present purpose.   The only point which concerns us here is, how far should the design be regulated by the limitations imposed by the craft itself?   If we have to put our windows

together like a mosaic by the use of "leads," it is obvious
that our design should be greatly
influenced by the leading, and in
all well-schemed windows the
design is largely outlined by these
leads, as a reference to any of the
examples given will demonstrate.
There are some leads which are
employed merely of necessity,
owing to the impossibility of cutting glass into very complicated
shapes; but these may be ignored,
as they do not interfere with our
principle, namely, that the leads
should so far as practicable outline
the design. The design should,
therefore, be simple and sculptu-
resque: a large style of design
should be chosen, and the attention should not be dissipated by a
wealth of trivialities.

A good instance of how skilfully the leads can be used in a
design is seen in the musical subject drawn by the late J. D.
Watson (Fig. 76). Here the design
is influenced all through by the
exigencies of the craft, and yet
there is a most successful union
between the craft and the design

Fig. 78. 'Charity.' One
of the Three Lights of
a Window in Christ
Church, Oxford. De-
signed by Sir E. Burne-
Jones, and executed by
Morris & Co.

an ideal marriage; for the very limitations imposed on the

designer have been accepted frankly, and turned to
account. This window was executed by Messrs. Campbell
Smith & Co.

In the filling of the lights of the window (Fig. 77), Messrs.
Guthrie, of Glasgow, have shown how much can be done

Fig. 79.—Part of a Window.   By Louis Davis.

with merely leading and the selection of beautiful glass, no
painting being done on the glass itself. By selecting choice
specimens of coloured glass for the "accents," and skilful
use of leads, much more may be done than most glass
stainers are aware of.

A third consideration in judging a window is that of
style : and here I am likely to tread on many tender places,

as more modern glass has been spoilt by a slavish adherence to antiquarianism than anything else. A thirteenth-century monk, when he fashioned a window for his monastery chapel, expressed himself as fully as his means would allow. He probably never drew directly from a model, but evolved his figures from his recollection. This monk was a beginner, and he had not museums of examples and photographs of other contemporary work to guide and help him. He was a pioneer journeying alone in an unknown country, and what wonder, therefore, if much that he did was like a learner's work? His implements also were of the simplest. The use of the diamond for cutting glass was unknown in the early days of glass painting, and he had to shape his piece of glass with a hot iron—a clumsy and uncertain method. But when all is said there can be no question that this monkish artist lived up to the knowledge of his time, and his work was only limited by his conditions; he did not wilfully impose limits upon himself. What shall we say, therefore, to those among us who ignore the advantages we possess—our facilities, our

Fig. 80. Boys Singing. Part of a Window by Louis Davis.

power of drawing, our extended palette, and who produce lifeless imitations of old work the letter without the spirit of the work they imitate, for those who follow others must always be behind—and then call their manufacture " thir teenth or fourteenth century glass," as though so labelled made it good *per se?* What we do should be nineteenth century, and I honour those men who have refused to produce archaic glass because the architect or donor of the window wished it, but have exhibited in their craft knowledge, and that individuality or character which *is* after all, as I have elsewhere insisted, "style."

Fig. 81.—Study.
By Louis Davis.

When the art of glass painting was revived, it was not surprising that to reproduce some of the best old windows was the only way to learn how to paint glass; but that is no reason why we should go on after forty years turning out modern old glass. Those acquainted with the glass in Oxford can see in Keble College Chapel windows of the archaic pattern; and in Christ Church glass which is, in the best sense, up-to-date. The former is manufacture, utterly uninteresting and wanting in beauty. In the Cathedral there is glass full of character and beauty, excellent in craftsmanship and design.

I give a small reproduction of "Charity," Fig. 78, one of three-light windows designed by Sir Edward Burne-Jones and executed by Morris & Co., whose glass gives the Cathedral great distinction.

All the Art crafts have suffered from manufacture. The individual is lost sight of in the "firm," just as though Art could be produced by a Co. ! The men who do the work

Fig. 82. Life Study for Cartoon
of a Window. By C. Whall.

Fig. 83. Finished Cartoon
for a Window. By C.
Whall.

are "hands," and the designers "cartoonists," who have just sufficient knowledge to draw conventional figures of saints after well-recognised patterns. It not infrequently happens that the "firm" does not have a fresh cartoon made for each window executed, but a head is taken, say, from St. Mark and put on the body of St. Luke; and by "fakes" of this nature a new design is the result, thereby saving money to the "firm," an ever-important consideration. The colouring of the window is either done in a purely arbitrary manner, or is left to the glazier, who, I am bound to admit, does not always do it as badly as might be.

Fig. 84. Part of Window.
By C. Whall.

Mr. C. Whall showed me a plan he adopts of making a small test window by sticking small pieces of the glass he thinks of using in his actual window on to a sheet of plate-glass, so that some idea of the colour effect can be obtained. But then Mr. Whall is an "artist" in stained glass, and not only draws his own cartoons, but chooses all the glass, and does much of the painting himself. Here art is not divorced from craftsmanship, and made into a manufacture; and no good work can ever be produced where the Art is lost sight of, and individuality merged in a company.

Fig. 85.   Window for a Library.   By Henry Ryland.

The drawing of a figure for a window should be as good as though it were for a picture; and as has already been said, only to wilfully reproduce the ignorance of a mediæval monk is to exhibit a shallow, misplaced veneration. But

the effects which a painter might legitimately strive for are not necessarily those which exhibit the art of the glass painter to the greatest advantage. He must realise that glass is not canvas, and that nothing must be attempted which destroys the brilliancy of his material. The less paint that is put on the glass the better (by paint I, of course, mean vitreous colours which require to be burnt on to the glass to make them permanent), and complicated actions necessitating subtle foreshortening should not be attempted, for this demands complicated chiaroscuro. An arm, for instance, held out towards one could not be adequately rendered in glass. A certain

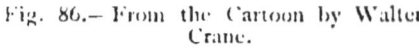

Fig. 86.— From the Cartoon by Walter Crane.

severity and restraint must keep the glass painter in check : in other words, his work must be conditioned by his opportunities.

The figure of "Charity" (Fig. 78) is, as I have said, one of three in a window at the north end of the north aisle of the cathedral at Oxford. The window is richly coloured, as light was not specially wanted from this window. The background is composed of foliage, and throws into relief the figures, but much is lost in the reproduction.

The large windows by the same artists in the east end of the building have much white glass, which is very skilfully employed, so that a due amount of light is admitted.

The name of Mr. Louis Davis is familiar to those who follow the progress of decorative art in this country, and the portions of three windows executed by him (Figs. 79, 80, and 81 here given speak for his ability as a designer for stained glass. Mr. Davis is particularly happy in his rendering of children, and the window of boys singing praises is as beautiful as anything executed in any age or country. The drawing is refined and scholarly, and is withal restrained, to fit it for its particular interpretation.

The reproduction of a cartoon for a window recently executed by Mr. C. Whall (Fig. 83), as well as the study from life for the same (Fig. 82), show that in his hands the craftsman and the artist are one. Mr. Whall takes great trouble in selecting his glass, and he adopts the excellent plan of making " palettes" of colour, as I have before mentioned, to gauge the effect of the window before it is carried out —a very different order of things to that which existed when I became a glass painter.

A good cartoon should be " glassy " from its first incep-

Fig. 87.— From the Glass by Walter Crane.
Executed by Mr. Sparrow.

tion. It is quite wrong to draw a window as you would an illustration, and then put the lead lines round it. The lead lines should largely *condition* the design. Madox Brown was the first artist in this century to realise this.

Mr. Henry Ryland is better known for his black-and-white work than for his purely decorative designing, but his window for a library (Fig. 85) exhibits his feeling for stained glass and his recognition of the necessities demanded by the craft. No strong colour is used, tinted whites and pale tones alone being employed.

Two illustrations are given of windows designed by Walter Crane and executed by Mr. Sparrow, for I hold that the student cannot have too many examples before him, provided they be good, as by this means he escapes the liability of falling into mannerism by being too much influenced by the work of one man. The cartoon by H. Ospovat Fig. 88 is one which took a prize at South Kensington in 1896. It shows that the author has realised the necessities to be observed.

In the chapter on "Women's Work" I have drawn attention to a particular make of glass which gives great "value" to a window owing to its thickness. This thick glass prevents a window looking poor or papery where much white or light glass is employed, and unless a window has a fair proportion of light glass in it, it not only keeps out light, but the requisite foil to the coloured glass is wanting. There is as much skill shown in the use of light and white glass in a window as there is in selecting the coloured portions. If glass is very thin it has a poor appearance when up, especially in the light parts, for the coloured portions are then in too strong opposition to the rest of the window. Some very beautiful glass is now

made, for much attention has been devoted to this part of
the work during the last ten years, and a glass painter
should bestow the greatest attention upon getting the best
material, for this is more than
half the battle in a successful
window. I am told that some
American firms have bestowed
even more attention to the make
of glass than we have, notably
Messrs. Tiffany, of New York,
for they have had pieces made
specially for particular portions
of a window. The result, if
artistically done, ought to be
very fine.

If any impression is left upon
the mind by a glance at the work
it has been my privilege to bring
before my readers, it is that a
new spirit is abroad which is
stimulating the men of to-day to
put into their work Art in place
of tradition, and thought in
place of convention; that in
their hands such a craft as that
of glass-painting is likely to be
carried further than we have
seen, and that windows will be

Fig. 88.—Cartoon for Glass.
By H. Ospovat.

painted which, for their beauty, will be a joy for ever. And
I would urge the clergy and all those who have the influence
in these matters to look round, take note of those men

Fig. 80. Windows in the Church of
the Ark of the Covenant, Stamford Hill.
Designed by Walter Crane, A.R.W.S.

The effect is entirely obtained by the leading, no painting being employed on the glass.

K

working as artists and not mechanics, and bestow upon them the patronage good work deserves. *Palmam qui meruit ferat,* which means that the patron should look out for the capable men when they are spending money on a stained-glass window, for instance, and see that what they are instrumental in putting into the church is worthy and of good report. Nothing is so discouraging as for the earnest worker to be left idle while the charlatan or mechanic is well employed. Many men will give from £500 to £1,000 for a portrait of themselves, and think that £100 quite enough to provide a painted window, though the cost of production in the latter case is many, many times what the painter has to spend on canvas and colours.

Fig. 90.—Stained Glass Panel in Door of Main Cabin. By G. C. Haité, R.B.A.

CHAPTER VIII.

WOOD CARVERS.

" Learn of sculptor, painter, poet,
     Take this lesson to thy heart :
That is best which lieth nearest,
     Carve from that thy work of art."
                    Longfellow.

"MAN is a tool-using animal "—"Sartor Resartus."
That being so, it is natural that wood-carving
has always been a popular craft with amateurs,
and one that played an important *rôle* among the Art crafts
of the Middle Ages, those glorious days for the "cunning"
worker in wood, metal, and stone. But it is weariness and
weakness to whimper over the days that are no more, so let
us take a brief survey of this craft of wood-carving as it
exhibits itself to us now. Nor is it any use going back to
the thirteenth century for our inspiration, and become slavish
reproducers of the work of that and the following century.
I hold strongly that what we have to do is to make the best
use of each moment as it goes by, for any attempt to return
to the past, and so lose touch of the present, is in the
long run putting the hands of the clock back. Much as I
respect Morris and acknowledge the influence he so benefi-
cially exerted on the crafts of the day, I cannot but help
feeling that in his printed books he made the initial mistake

of ignoring the *zeitgeist.* Had he brought his genius to bear upon the *format* of books, he might have levelled up the art of printing so that all would have benefited, whereas by reproducing books in the style of the fifteenth century we can only view his efforts as interesting experiments lying quite outside the march of mankind.

Wood carving suffers much from the heavy hand of the past, which presses upon the work of to-day and robs it of vitality. This is especially true of ecclesiastical carving, which always has to be in some "style." originality being the last quality desired. In the carving in a church how much more interesting would be the result if, say, a dozen craftsmen were turned loose, each to work out his artistic salvation, so to say, there ; instead of some "Master" or church furnisher taking on the job and employing a designer to make the drawings and so many "hands" at so much an hour to do the work, the profit and the *kudos* going to the firm.

If those who spend money on churches would try to be as artistic as they are pious, and see that their money is spent to some worthy end in securing original work by capable craftsmen, how much gain would accrue! Our churches might then be living temples instead of crystallisations of the past or receptacles of "furniture" art.

I was much struck, at the last Arts and Crafts Exhibition, at some carved pew ends in low relief by Mr. H. Wilson. They were in perfect harmony and yet distinctly of to-day, the work of a man who had his own outlook, who could learn of the past and yet be of the present.

It is the dead uniformity of modern church work—"the No. 6, page 99 of 'our' catalogue"—which so dulls the

Fig. 61.   Part of the Bishop's Throne, St. Paul's Cathedral.   Carved by W. Aumonier.

senses of the beholder and makes him pass by unheeding instead of enjoying the "joy of the working." Considering what an important patron the church still is, it grieves one to see the lamentable waste of money in purchasing work which, as art, is valueless. Ecclesiastical correctness (whatever that may mean) is thought more of than imagination and skilful originality. The late J. D. Sedding set a good example by seeking out clever painters and sculptors and craftsmen to enrich the fabric he designed.

Let us hear what wood-carvers have to say touching their

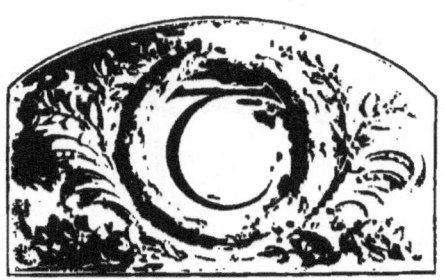

Fig. 92.—Carved Panel.   By W. Aumonier.

work, and the patronage extended to them, and I think I cannot do better than turn to a symposium of craftsmen who addressed a meeting of the Royal Institute of British Architects early this year, and give the gist of what Messrs. Romaine-Walker, W. Aumonier, J. E. Knox, and W. S. Frith had to tell their audience of architects, who are, of necessity, brought much in contact with wood-carvers.

Mr. Romaine-Walker represented the architect-patron, and he touched the keynote when he said : " Woodcarving, being an art, the very nature of which brings it within the reach of the million, and, as it were, into their daily life, has been, perhaps, the first to suffer from over-production, and consequent decline. The mind of the public has

only too often exposed for sale in shops, and praised by the employés, who affect a critical faculty entirely foreign to their nature and bringing-up. To the vast majority of mankind these vacuous salesmen are the oracles of public taste ; it therefore follows that much of the delicacy of perception which our forefathers possessed has been lost." And when the speaker had to refer to the relations which should exist between architect and carver, he laid it down as a principle that, while directing and supervising the work, he should, like the playwright, after having painted in words the lesson or impression he wishes to convey, leave the exponent of his thoughts certain liberty of action, else will he take from the executed work its soul, and leave it but a lifeless production. Under the influence of the Gothic architects wood-carving was the handmaid of architecture.

It is a pity that this just principle should not influence architects more than it does in their treatment of their "handmaids." There is such a slavish adherence to precedent on the part of many architects, which makes them tie down the craftsman until his ego is squeezed out of him. I am reminded that I walked into Keble College chapel the other day, to look again at the decoration, and if the architect takes the responsibility for the hideous painted windows and mosaic panels, he has taken upon himself an Atlas load indeed !

Mr. Aumonier, the next speaker, referred to the way the wood-carver in the past was evolved out of the village carpenter, as is seen in the "choppy, vigorous cut of the Chester and Ambrosio work at Milan, the carver having only just emerged from the use of the chisel proper to take

up the carver's gouge." Wood-carving should not be made
to represent marble, bronze, silver, or any other material,
for, by the very individuality of its treatment, it may attain
a charm and beauty equal to that of almost any substance
the hand of man can fashion. " To this end we want it cut
by a strong man fully alive to the capabilities and suscepti-
bilities of his material. If he is a good workman, he will
combine freshness and grace ; freshness because the work
grows under his own hand, showing the cuts and gouge-

Fig. 94.- Carved Panel. By George Jack.

marks in it freely and fearlessly to the last, to mark for ever
the secret of its birth like the last strokes of the painter's
brush ; grace, because there is no form the artistic mind can
conceive but may be obtained in wood, if honestly sought
after."

This carver's word to architects is " to treat their carver
as a brother artist or craftsman, in sympathy with the work
in hand, called in to give artistic finish to new buildings,
and not as a person out of whom is to be screwed as much

work as possible, for as small an amount of money as the carver will allow his patrons to give him."

Mr. W. Aumonier was apprenticed to a firm of furniture manufacturers and general decorators, the foreman of the wood-carvers being Mr. Mark Rogers, "one of the most skilful and artistic carvers we have had in modern times." Then he worked with a Belgian sculptor settled in

Fig. 95.—Central Panel in Italian Walnut.   By George Jack.

Westminster, and after that in Paris, working in both wood and stone, and for six months on the restoration of Amiens Cathedral, under M. Viollet le Duc.   This gave our craftsman a decided penchant for architectural work, as distinct from mere cabinet carving, and the stone carving of such buildings as the new municipal offices at Oxford is as important a part of this craftsman's work as the woodcarving he executed for St. Paul's Cathedral.   Mr. Aumonier roughs out the designs in charcoal for his craftsmen. leaving the interpretation to them, and he much deprecates not only the waste of money caused by modelling the designs previous to carving them in wood, but the tendency to make the carver mechanical, a mere imitating machine instead of an artist. His method of study has been to go direct to old work, sketching it for himself so as to feel the spirit of the old craftsman, and not to rely upon books of examples drawn by other men ; very sensible advice. I take it, and equivalent to the drawing from nature instead of from copies.

Fig. 96. Our Lady of the Rood. By Harry Hems.

Mr. J. E. Knox said that his craft had been striving during the last thirty years to raise itself above the cabinet and upholstery incubus under which it had fallen for many generations, and efforts have been made by the establishment of the British Wood-Carvers' Society a body of craftsmen far too little known by kindred societies to regain the position wood-carving held in the seventeenth and eighteenth centuries. " Wood-carving is an absorbing, fascinating, but a time-taking occupation, and the results of his labour are, as a rule, gratifying to the executant, whatever his architect or client may subsequently think of his work."

The speaker went on to say that it was by studying the work in some of our cathedrals and old churches that he liberated himself from a certain petty egotism from which he suffered at the outset of his career. " I carved birds, flowers, miniature figures and many pretty things besides, and although greatly admired, no one wanted to buy them."

The choppiness of late fifteenth-century work, Mr. Knox said, was a powerful influence in his development, for he admired the *gee* in this style of carving, and the apparent fact that the carvers knew when they had done enough to their work. As examples for the wood-carver to study, this craftsman gives the following :—

> Norman Zigzag, Rochester Cathedral.
> Early English, 11th and 12th Centuries, Choir, Westminster Abbey.
> Decorated, 13th and 14th Centuries, Lady Chapel, Ely, and Choir, York Minster.
> Perpendicular, 14th and 15th Centuries, King's College, Cambridge.
> Tudor, 1550 to 1600, Thornbury Castle, Gloucester.
> Jacobean, 1600 to 1650, Longleat House, Wilts.

Mr. Knox is one instance, out of many, of a craftsman of deservedly high reputation, who worked into art for himself and in spite of most adverse circumstances, for being left an orphan, when barely nine years old, he obtained a berth at a West-end cabinet firm to glasspaper up carvings and run errands. The hours were from seven till seven, but in spite of this the young enthusiast took possession of a disused attic, got a few tools, and rigged up

Fig. 97.— Carving in Oak. Carved by J. E. Knox. Designed by Stephen Webb.

a bench in order to attain his ambition of becoming a wood-carver. He became sufficiently proficient to be taken, at the age of fourteen, by the master carver as an apprentice without premium and with the wages he was receiving as errand boy; and when out of his time worked for seven years for Mr. Thomas Earp, the architectural sculptor, and it is Mr. Knox's advice to would-be carvers to be apprenticed to an architectural carver rather than to a cabinet firm.

Fig. 98.   Clock Case in Chestnut Wood.   By Mark Rogers.

Having worked for some of the leading architects, Mr. Knox attributes the progress in decorative art during the last thirty years to that brilliant band of young architects who, when he was a young man, struggled so manfully to elevate public taste in matters architectural.

Mr. W. S. Frith also laments the want of discriminating patronage denied the wood carver. "It is a little difficult to understand in these days," he says, "that there seems

Fig. 99. Panel at back of the Bishop's Throne, St. Paul's Cathedral. Carved by W. Aumonier.

little demand for choice wood-carving beyond the foliage order; no doubt this is in great part due to the fact that wood sculpture does not conveniently lend itself to production from the clay modelling point of view, from which most sculptors, both here and abroad, are trained."

All the speakers were agreed that wood-carving should never be a copy of a modelled design, for there is required an essential treatment of the wood, which makes wood-carving differ from other crafts. "While oak is the principal wood for carving, others have to be considered; and if the treatment of oak were, for instance, applied to satin-wood, the result would be to make the satin-wood look very much like pine. In this case the work looks most precious when it is so designed and carved as to permit the opalescent quality of the wood to sing through the carving."

All the speakers again were agreed as to marks of the tool showing, and that to get the finish of *carton-pierre* was destructive of the finest qualities in wood-carving. In Mr. Frith's words, "the question of how far the cutting of the wood should be evident—as a general rule, figure form is most satisfactory with the tool marks invisible; since the form is the essential, not the manner of producing it: and this rule necessarily applies wherever exact form is desired. The clear cut, however, best displays the quality of the material, the mastery of the craftsman, and his delight in his work, and makes that in which the dexterous use of the tool can be traced one of the most charming phases of wood-carving."

In these remarks of eminent craftsmen may be gleaned the *Sophia* as opposed to the *Moria*, as Ruskin would say, of the art. On that crucial question of style it seems to me that, both from their words and works, wood-carvers are too much afraid of expressing their ego. Mr. Frith says that the yearning to invent something new is particularly fascinating to the mind of youthful cast, and seemed to question whether, "with so great a mass of past experience influencing us," this novelty was attainable. Yet, when wood-carvers speak of our great Grinling Gibbons, it is always as scholars towards an honoured master, and Gibbons's work stands the test of centuries for its individuality, as much as for its technical excellence. No repetition of past work either invigorates or develops our present efforts. Mr. Mark Rogers, Jun., received his first instruction from his father, and for ten years was in the life class at Lambeth, and before beginning work on his own account spent a year in the South Kensington Museum School. The human figure enters largely into his designs, as it did in that of

Fig. 100. Birmingham School of Handicraft.

Grinling Gibbons (as witness his screen in the chapel of Trinity College, Oxford); and though I have heard

it said that wood is not a good material to use for
figure carving, the human form, when well drawn and
composed, adds greatly to the interest of the craft.   The
supporting figures for the chimney-pieces at Ashridge (and
which were exhibited in the Royal Academy in 1886, 1887,
and 1890) were carved by Mr. Rogers.   Many of our
younger sculptors are turning their attention to decorative
work, and it would seem that the dividing line which has
hitherto kept apart sculptors and carvers is being rubbed
away.   It is time this was so.   Alfred Stevens did not
disdain to carve mantelpieces, and a sculptor's energies
might be better applied to the decoration of a room or
building than carving busts of middle-aged gentlemen with
bald heads and nicely brushed whiskers.

The work of Mr. George Jack I first saw at the "Arts
and Crafts."   He represents the newer influences which
have stimulated our craftsmen and taken them out of the
rut of precedent.   Professional wood-carvers allude to much
of the work there exhibited as the "rabbit-hutch" school,
and the striving for originality has a tendency to produce
eccentricity, but the endeavour on the part of the committee
to give the first place to original work is a right one, though
they cannot be too eclectic in choosing the works to exhibit,
and so avoid an impression of monotony which is slightly
observable in certain crafts.

The School of Art Wood-carving has shifted its quarters
from the Albert Hall to the Central Technical College,
Exhibition Road.   It has the advantage of being a teaching
body as well as a society of workers.   The example of
their work given is by W. H. Grimwood, one of the
instructors to the school.   The fees vary from £5 a quarter

for day tuition, to £2 for evening tuition, the students providing their own tools and materials.

The Birmingham School of Handicraft is a young society, and, from the examples of their work, I should say has vitality and earnestness to stimulate it, and keep it on the stretch. Why is it, by the way, that Brummagen is used as

Fig. 101. Carved Oak Settle. (Southwold School of Handicraft.)

a term of reproach? Is it because mechanical finish, the result of the factory system, has become so hateful in our eyes? The town has shown considerable activity in the matter of art to remove the reproach, but art cannot thrive in factories, where the individual is merely the cog to a wheel in the huge machine.

I fancy that carvers do not sufficiently realise that hand cunning does not make a piece of work a work of art. Manipulative skill must be directed to some worthy end, and be kept within bounds by selection and appreciation of line and mass. So much wood-carving lacks distinction : it is no better than high-class manufacture through wanting the charm of personality. I would sooner have less hand-cunning and more personality, though there is no reason why the one should not be added to the other. Amateurs find wood-carving a craft peculiarly suited to them because it employs the fingers, and they can watch their work grow under their hands, and they soon get a sense of power over their material. One friend, an en-

Fig. 102.—Working Design for Cabinet.
H. D. Richter.
(Prize Design, South Kensington.)

gineer, has carved a complete set of dining-room furniture, including a very massive sideboard. He gets his designs from bits of old carving he takes rubbings of, and fits them together into some sort of " whole." Could he but import a little touch of originality into his work how much it would gain ! If he, instead of going into a church for his inspiration, went out to nature, drew let us say some familiar form like the bramble, and then adapted it to his requirements, he would be giving us himself as well as his finger dexterity. He, like many others, thinks too little of the design and too much of the carving. A certain ruggedness, a vigorous spontaneity would be better than the impersonal refinement which many amateurs appear to think is the only quality to go for. It is something like the man who gave so much attention as to how to speak and use his voice that he quite forgot how little he had to say when he was ready to say it.

I am glad to be able to give an example of work done under the influence of the Society for the Encouragement of Village Industries and Craftsmanship. The settle (Fig. 101), which was shown last year at the annual exhibition at the Albert Hall, is a straightforward piece of work evidently modelled after the old oak chests which have the last few years been so prized by those who love that which is of good report.

CHAPTER IX

BOOKBINDERS.

Fig. 103.—Design for Binding. By the Co-operative Bookbinders.

CRAFT of bookbinding has during the last dozen years been invaded, or perhaps I had better say followed, by several amateurs, who have gained for themselves some distinction as binders, as well as calling the attention of booklovers to the desirability of investing the designs of bookbindings with individuality, instead of repeating those *motifs* which have been used time after time until all interest in them has departed. Women have taken to the craft with much success, as these pages can testify, and it certainly is a calling well within the compass of many women who, having taste and some skill in designing, will go through the apprenticeship necessary to acquire the technique.

Bindings have occupied a prominent place in the shows of the "Arts and Crafts" in former exhibitions, though less so in the last one, and many an old binder must have rubbed his eyes to assure himself that the daring manner of the "tooling," as well as the prices asked for "such eccentricities," were really what he saw before him. "I'd be an artistic bookbinder if I got such prices," I think I can hear him say. Perhaps if the old binder had given *his* bindings that spice of originality which so staggered him in the work of the exhibitors at the "Arts and Crafts," he too might have obtained increased prices for his work, for people are prepared to pay for originality ; it is mediocrity that comes off so poorly.

In selecting the illustrations to accompany this chapter I have given representative bindings of what may be, for the sake of distinction, called the old school, from the library of Mr. S. A. Thompson Yates, who was kind enough to lend me the books here figured, and a series of bindings by Mr. Cobden-Saunderson, who is thoroughly representative of the modern spirit, as well as a few others ; and I have also shown the work of a local handicraft class started by a lady some four years or so since, to show how much may be done by reviving the art instincts dormant throughout the country, and diverting this activity brought into play so that it does not dissipate itself in unworthy works. Other examples of the work wrought under the stimulus of the Home Arts and Industries Association will be found in this work.

Mr. Cobden-Saunderson's atelier is opposite the Kelm-

scott Press, where William Morris set up his printing-press
and produced those books, such as "Chaucer," that he
evidently hoped would stem the tide which, from his point

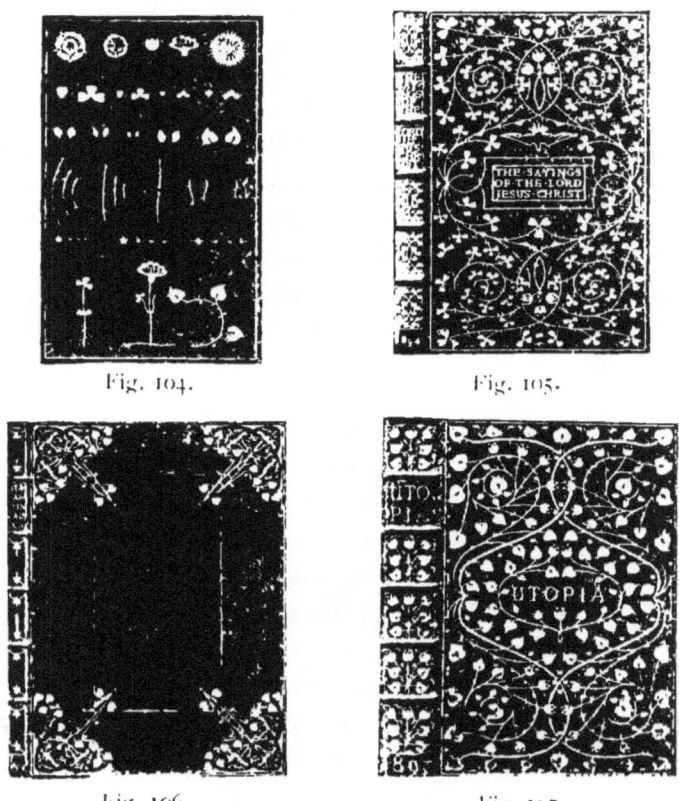

Fig. 104.   Fig. 105.

Fig. 106   Fig. 107.

Fig. 104.   Impressions of Tools.   Figs. 105, 106, 107.—Bindings.
By Mr. C. J. Cobden-Saunderson.

of view, swept away all distinction in modern printing. It
is a delightful bit of old London, the Upper Mall, and a
refreshing contrast to that feverishly-active and blatant part

of Hammersmith adjoining, where so much effort is expended in the attempt to make the public believe they can purchase two penny buns for three-ha'pence.

I take Mr. Cobden Saunderson as a representative binder

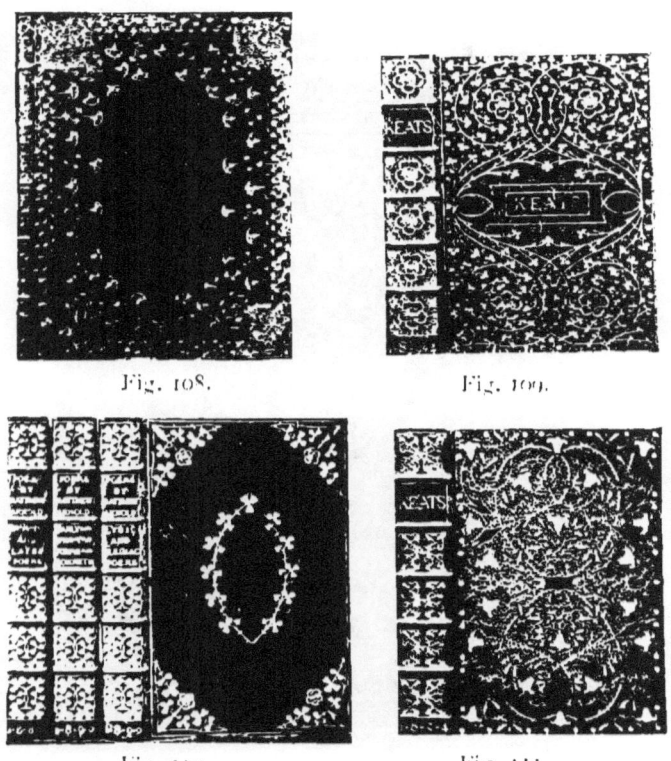

Fig. 108.   Fig. 109.

Fig. 110.   Fig. 111.

Figs. 108, 109, 110, 111. Bindings. By Mr. C. J. Cobden-Saunderson.

because he has stepped out of the groove of tradition, has impressed his individuality upon his work in the way that old Roger Payne did over a century ago, and has brought thought and love to the craft he has chosen to follow, so that the work turned out by him is the very best of its kind.

Mr. Cobden-Saunderson's life story, so far as it concerns

Fig. 112.— Binding. By Mr. Birdsall, of Nottingham.

us here, is briefly told. After being a barrister for some years, he left the Bar and went for six months with Roger De Coverley to learn "forwarding," working as an ordinary "hand" the while. After that he opened a workshop over

Messrs. Williams and Norgate in Maiden Lane. The next move was to convert his own drawing-room into an atelier, and for seven years he worked at binding books and decorating their covers with patterns, his wife doing the sewing.

Fig. 113. Binding. By "Roger de Coverley."

In those days Cobden-Saunderson and his wife did every part of the work, but some two years ago he rented a house at Hammersmith, took into his employ three or four workmen and a girl to do the sewing, and so established the "Doves Bindery."

Bookbinding divides itself into three departments: one, the sewing of the pages together securely and in such a way that the book can be opened with comfort; two, the putting of the book between protective boards or covers; and three, the ornamenting of these covers with patterns. A well-bound book should be practically indestructible, and the sewing is, therefore, done by hand, whereas books as they are issued to the public (save in a few exceptional instances) are sewed by machinery, and frequently now with wire instead of string.

Mr. Cobden-Saunderson is as particular about this part of the work as the ornamenting of the covers, for while the "tooling" is a matter entirely optional, the sewing and "forwarding" is one of necessity, and a bookbinder would first of all look at the "back" of a book and see how it opened before he would examine its ornamentation. In the days when books were few they were such highly cherished possessions that great attention was paid to the binding and the decoration of the covers, as a glance at the cases in the King's Library in the British Museum testifies. These bindings must have been very costly, and it is in this spirit of veneration for books that some few among us spend, what seems to those content with shilling editions of the classics, an outrageous sum for binding a few of their literary treasures. Such were the examples Cobden-Saunderson, like other bookbinders, had before him when he began. But just as the vitality of peoples dies out through lack of fresh blood, so schools of design, living always upon themselves, soon lack vitality, and die finally of inanition; tradition, therefore, ceases to be a teaching influence.

I asked Mr. Cobden-Saunderson how he learnt designing, and he replied that the faculty was gradually developed, that he began by dividing the surface to be ornamented into spaces, and filling each space with some
simple *motif* like a trefoil. "When I got one foot planted
I put the other down, and so began my journey." It was
useless, he felt, working on old lines; he must tread out
a path for himself, and that he has done so a glance
at this binder's work proves. All designs should have
a geometrical basis and should follow a well-ordered
plan, and that method of treating a book-cover as a
Japanese does a fan, does not commend itself to this master binder; for, as Mr. Cobden-Saunderson said to me, it
was his desire "to set himself in symmetrical harmony with.
the things around him."

All designs should be merely a development of the
simple use of the tools used, and a glance at the impressions made by the tools on the cover (Fig. 104) will
explain what is meant better than many words. With
just these few tools endless combinations are possible, and
they may be considered in the same relation to book-cover
decoration as the notes in the scale are in music. Mr.
Saunderson holds that the fewer the tools used in book-
cover decoration the better. The skill should be exhibited
in the pleasing and infinite combinations of a few *motifs*,
and if the examples of his bindings be examined, it
will be found that though great richness of effect is
obtained, the resources are few, as in the binding of the
book, "The Sayings of the Lord Jesus Christ" (Fig. 105).

Some bibliophiles urge that there should be some relation
between the cost of the binding and the value of the book

itself. My friend Mr. Thompson Yates objects to binding
a 6s. edition of Tennyson in a £6 binding, but in the case
of a rare or unique copy of a book such an expenditure on
the binding may be justified. Mr. Saunderson, when I
put this to him, said that this is a fallacy, for the value of a
book does not depend upon the cost of its paper and the
machine-printing, but upon its value as a work of genius.

Fig. 114. - Inlaid Binding.   By " Roger de Coverley."

He binds a book, the best of its kind procurable, and
though the poems of Keats may be purchased for a few
shillings, there is no reason why you should not honour
the poet by binding his works at a cost of many pounds.
The further question of the cost of his bindings touches a
delicate topic, for Mr. Cobden-Saunderson's bindings have
run to as much as from £20 to £40 per volume. Few can

pay this price, but then few can buy pictures or any other supreme work of men's hands; but if they who, out of the margin of their incomes, like to bind books they greatly value absolutely as well as they can be bound, the world is certainly the gainer, for man being, as Carlyle says, a tool-using animal, nothing interests him more than

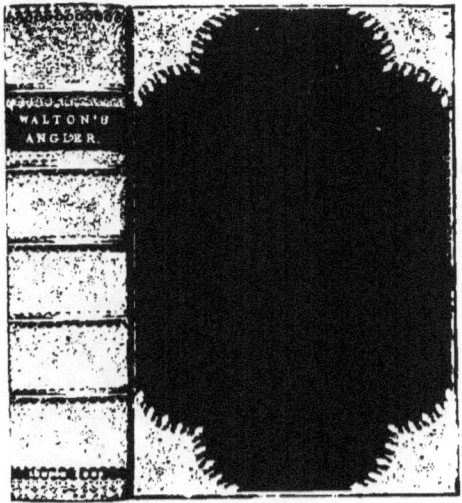

Fig. 115.—Binding. By Fazakerley.

to see skilful craftsmanship the perfection of hand-cunning.

It seems to me worth while here to quote a few sentences from what I may call the master binder's decalogue, for in the papers contributed by Mr. Cobden-Saunderson to present-day literature are some very luminous thoughts on Art crafts generally, binding in particular.

1. "A half-bound book is an economy, and economy is incompatible with decoration."

2. "We should not enshrine in a beautiful binding the ephemeral productions of the moment."

3. "The beautiful book, the work of genius, the immortal in literature, should be the exclusive object of the binder's craft when heightened by the art of the decorator. The

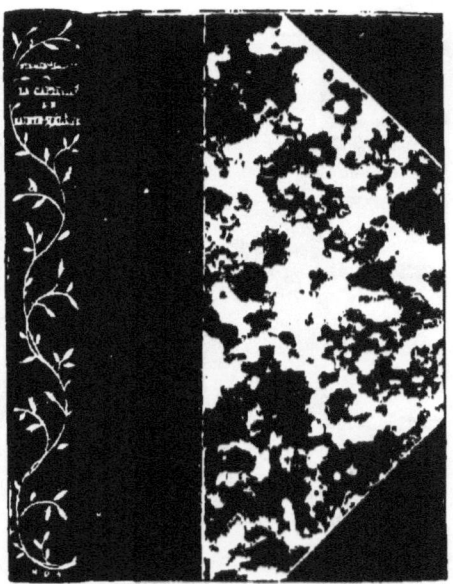

Fig. 116.— Half-bound Book.   By the Co-operative Bookbinders.

decoration should be done in honour of him whose genius it should be a delight to honour."

4. "Shall I ever attain to such skill, to such consciousness of power, that I shall not even know *how* to fail?"

5. "Wholly to achieve victory in the binder's craft, to forget no end in the prosecution of the means, to exaggerate no feature from long practice and perfect skill, to permit

no craft of hand to overcome the judgment of the head, is in this, as in all crafts, an exceedingly difficult task."

6. " He can 'tool,' but he cannot design : and he has so

CHASTE
-LARD·A
TRAGEDY
A·C·SWIN-
-BURNE

CHAS
-TE-
LARD

1894
LONDON

Fig. 117.- Design for Binding. By Messrs. Dent & Co.

magnified execution that when completely successful, when completely triumphant, he is then most conspicuously a failure ! "

M

7. "What an education the prosecution of a craft is for the soul of a man! The silent matter which is the craftsman's material is wholly in his hands; it hears and makes no reproaches, but it never forgives and it has no mercy."

8. "Design is invention and development, and when development has reached a certain point the invention is exhausted, and some new departure must be taken. No new departure has been taken since the three historic schools closed."

9. "In the first place there must be in every design a scheme or framework of distribution; the area to be covered must be covered according to some symmetrical plan. The scheme or framework of distribution must itself be covered by the orderly repetition and, if need be, modification and development of some primary element of decoration, which we may call a *motif*. All patterns to be good must be organic in the relation of their details, and organic in the method of their development."

10. "It is in the intention of the harmony of the universe that the ideal of the work of the hand resides. It is in itself an adjustment at once beautiful and serviceable. It is a dedication of man's powers to an end not beyond man's reach. It is in this wise that I commend to you all the life of the workman, of the workman working in little in the spirit of the whole."

I leave Mr. Cobden-Saunderson's work to speak for itself. That he is faithful to his creed is evident by the examples given, though the beauty of the tooling cannot be shown in the illustrations, only the plan of the design.

A book design may be made symbolical of the contents,

as in the example of Mr. Birdsall of Nottingham, Fig. 112,
the Gothic character of the design harmonizing with Street's
" Gothic Architecture in Spain."

This and the examples of " Roger de Coverley " and
Fazakerley of Liverpool are from Mr. Thompson Yates'
library, and are all excellent examples of tooling, and in
some cases inlaying ; Fig. 114, *i.e.*, where parts of the design
have small pieces of other coloured leather let in, such inlays
being glued down to the covers, and tooled so as to incor-
porate them into the general design. But the beauty of
these, as of all bindings, must be *felt* to be appreciated.

The design, Fig. 117, of Messrs. Dent & Co., reminds me
that Mr. Dent, who kindly took me over his workshops, produces commercial bindings which have some distinction, as
the binder who tools them works out his own ideas in each
cover, so that no two are quite alike. The super-superior
person may sneer at this and carp at the result, but he
might remember that the majority of us cannot often
indulge in a ten-shilling binding, and to make the average
binder an artist is after all the direction all effort should
take. By the side of this binder of Mr. Dent's was a
machine stitching his shilling edition of the plays of
Shakespeare, the covers of which are, of course, wholly
the product of a machine, the only hand-work being the
gluing of the covers on to each play.

Miss Bassett has kindly supplied me with examples, Fig.
118, of the leather work done by the Leighton Buzzard handicraft class, which she was instrumental in starting some four
or five years ago. " My class was started originally with the
object of giving employment to a crippled child in the town.
There are now some six or seven cripples who work regu-

larly at binding and leather work.   And these are paid by

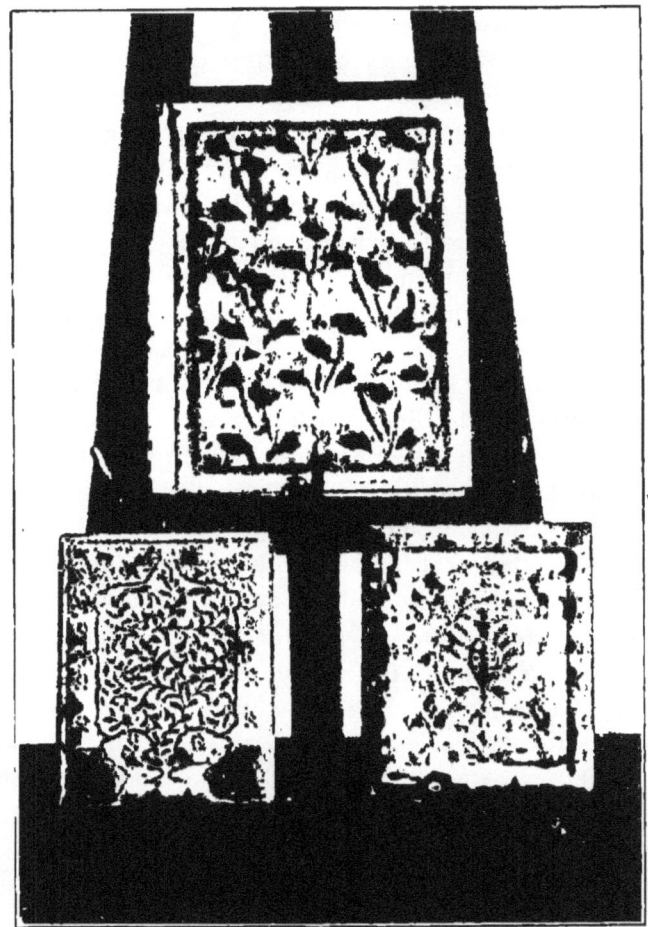

Fig. 118.—Bindings.   By Miss Bassett.

the hour according to the excellence of their work.   Our
method of tooling the leather is much the same as that

adopted in the German bindings, but our speciality is that of tinting and gilding the leather after it is embossed."

From the work I have seen I judge it to be good of its kind, especially as workmanship. Embossed or beaten-up leather is a favourite method with Miss Bassett's craftsmen, and very beautiful effects can be obtained by this means. This beaten leather work, almost identical in method with repoussé metal-work, is being more and more employed by

Fig. 119.—Printed Book-Cover Design. Adaptation of natural plan form. By B. A. Waldram.

contemporary binders, and with excellent results in many cases.

A word may be said with regard to the designs for ordinary cloth bindings, seeing that some of our best decorative artists work for the trade binders ; for nothing is more cheering than to find it worth the while of commerce to engage the services of artists. "We have got on," as Mr. Egerton Bompas said in Mr. Pinero's comedy, when this is to be noted, as it may be by any one who looks at the bindings of books issued by our leading publishers, and compares them with those of half-a-dozen years since.

The design by B. A. Waldram, Fig. 119, is one which gained a prize at South Kensington, and shows considerable ingenuity in the management of intricate lines.

I may here say that I am responsible for the design of the cover of this book. I aimed at a severe simplicity, for the method of producing these bindings seems to suggest that, but at the same time I wanted to get a direct reference to nature in the design, which is suggested, as the reader can see, by the Columbine (A. Crysantha). I know of few things that exercise one's taste and ingenuity more than a cloth-cover design. You get none of the choiceness which comes of tooling, and therefore your effect must be obtained in quite a different way to that of the binder, and it is better therefore to steer quite away from such effects.

I cannot do better than close this chapter by giving some extracts from an article on "A New Technique in Tooling," contributed by Mr. D. S. MacColl to *The Art Journal.* The writer's remarks are a distinct contribution to the subject, for they not only advocate what I insist upon (my readers will say *ad nauseam*)—the development of the individuality and the breaking up of new ground instead of going on tilling soil which has become sterile by over-cropping, but they point with definiteness to a fresh treatment of tooling, as can be seen by the specimens of the bindings executed by Miss MacColl under her brother's tutelage.

"The designing of the first books led me to speculate on the curious limits under which tooling has been done for hundreds of years. What these limits are must be familiar to many people from a number of recent books and articles on the subject, so that it will be unnecessary to go into the matter at length. The early type of cover decoration was of a different sort. Blocks, running from a small to a considerable size, and in character like the dies used to stamp medals or seals, were employed to stamp a whole device at one blow in a press, and to render it in raised relief. The devices were symbolic, heraldic, or illustrative. In the later type, surviving with many changes of style to our day, instead of freely designing a block in one piece to decorate his cover, the binder builds a design for each book out of a number of hand tools which can be re-combined. These tools impress themselves in sunk relief, and the impression is frequently gilded. They divide up into four sorts :—

1. *The Wheels or ' Fillets.'*—These wheels are employed to draw the straight lines bounding the cover or framing smaller panels.

2. *The Curves or ' Gouges.'*—For every curved line, on the other hand, and for every separate length of curved line, as well as for short straight lines, an individual tool is cut out.

3. *The Stamps.*—These are small tools cut into the form of spirals, leaves, flowers, dots, stars, and any other shapes required in addition to curved and straight lines.

4. *Rolls* and *Pallets* are wheels and segments on which is impressed a running recurring pattern.

The different styles of the bookbinders have differed considerably in the importance of the part assigned to each class of tool. Some have preferred lines straight and curved, others have mingled lines and stamps in elaborate design, others have "powdered" their surfaces with stamps or grouped them in tiny lace-work patterning.   The old

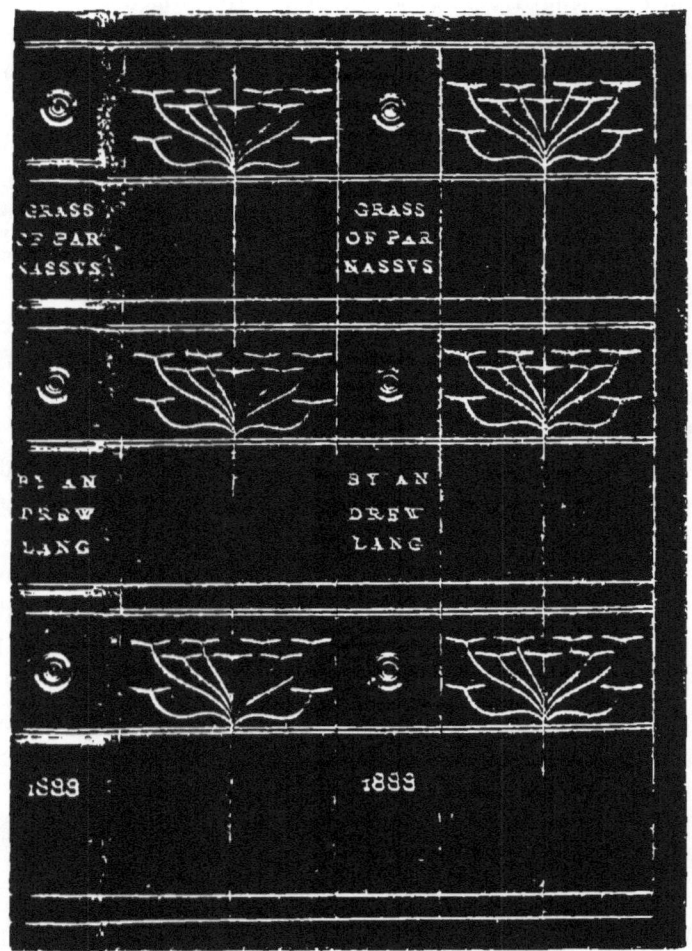

Fig. 120.—MacColl binding for " Grass of Parnassus."
By Andrew Lang.

press-blocks or " plaques " have frequently been revived in

combination with the new tooling. The only accepted technique permitting some freedom of drawing with the stock tools has been the marking out of forms with a dot.

Fig. 121.— MacColl binding to a copy of W. H. Pater's "The Renaissance."

It is sometimes argued that this technical tradition in the matter of tools imposes a valuable check on the taste with which designs are made—affects them with a certain restraint and control. The argument, I fear, is doubly fallacious. A man without taste can produce results as horrible with a few lines and curves as if he had all the forms in the world to choose from. But the supposed check is really no check at all. The only limit is the number of curves and stamps that a binder chooses or can afford to have cut for each book, and a survey of modern binding will show how absolutely without influence on style is this tradition of technique. It is true, of course, that there is something amusing in the attempt to obtain numerous combinations out of an arbitrarily limited set of forms : this ingenious and acrobatic side of design has its fascination. But where taste and ingenuity are wanting, nothing will come of a negative check but a geometrical re-shuffling : where these qualities are present they can be safely left to determine their own limits, and will determine them with an inherent severity much stricter than any arbitrarily imposed.

Is there, then, any point at which this tradition of tool-making might be relaxed with advantage, so as to allow the decorator to arrive more easily at results he already makes shift to reach in spite of it? There is surely one such very obvious modification. Already, in drawing straight lines, the binder employs a tool, namely, the wheel, which might with equal reason be employed in drawing curves. This tool is in the binder's hands; there would appear to be something superstitious in objecting to its extended use. The advantages of its use may be summarised as economy of means with variety of effect. Thus : —

1. All the curves already produced by rigid tools can be

executed by a wheel, and even many of the smaller forms
for which stamps are commonly cut.

2. In practice, when a binder does not have tools
specially cut to carry out a design, but re-combines a set of
stock tools, the curves he employs are the simpler and
stricter curves, chiefly segments of circles of various radii.
To get anything near the play and delicacy of curvature
that a draughtsman would naturally introduce into a line
design, the stock of segment curves would have to be
enormous, both in variety of length and of radius; nor
would there appear to be any reason in the nature of things
why the curves on a book-cover must be of this segmentary
character. The wheel, a single tool, displaces all this
apparatus, and allows of delicacies of inflection beyond
what the largest stock of fixed curves could execute. In
fact, it puts a pencil into the hand of the book-decorator,
a natural counterpart of the tool used by the designer.
The economy of means may be illustrated from Fig. 121, the
design for Mr. Pater's " Renaissance." The curved stem-
lines in these instances, simple as they are, do not fall
among the segmental curves usually supplied to the
bookbinder, and had, therefore, to be expressly cut for the
purpose. With the wheel these lines can be readily drawn.
An examination of the remaining designs will show how
much ease and freedom of curvature are possible in this
new technique. Thus the lines of the peacock's tail could
be readily reproduced without any anxious fitting of stock
curves to the lines, or the making of new tools expressly to
render them. The wheels, it should be explained, which
are employed in straight-line drawing have a diameter of
several inches, a convenience when a long line has to be

drawn, and also because equable pressure comes more easily with a heavier tool, and heat is retained longer by a larger tool. But these large wheels could not turn within a small angle, and our innovation consisted in having a small wheel constructed with a diameter less than that of a threepenny piece. With this all but very sharp turns are possible, and these can be managed with the additional resource of few links and joints. With this apparatus, as a reference to the designs will show, it is possible to execute forms of considerable intricacy, though we have not, in these illustrations, by any means pressed its powers to their limits. The use of the wheel, it should be added, calls for a certain power of drawing in its handler, in the sense of being able to follow a line, freehand, with swing and nicety.

The tradition of design in bookbinding is only at certain points respectable, the amount of original talent devoted to it having been small. Now, the governing considerations that make a design fundamentally good or bad are, in binding as in other arts, not the elegance of this or that detail, but the plan and scale of the whole design and the logical beauty with which the parts are compacted or grow from one another. The plan of having a number of stock tools mechanically re-combined frequently defeats the operation of such a sense, since a series of curves and of details cut for one size of cover will seldom fit another. The real "limits" of design for bindings are severe enough. The planning should be governed by the fact that not only the spaces of the two sides must be considered, but also the six panels into which the back is divided by its bands, or, if there are no bands, the single slim panel of the

Fig. 122.   MacColl binding of Catalogue of the Arts and Crafts
Exhibition, 1889.   Peacock and Fountain.

back.   The breadth of the back should affect throughout
the scale of ornament.

A further complication enters with the title. If a title is put on the back, the scale of lettering adopted in it determines the scale of ornament throughout. This is the real crux of bookbinders' designing, and it is obvious how often designers evade it by attempting no relation between the scale of ornament on the back and on the sides. But if there are bands on the back, as must inevitably be the case in the best flexible work, design is still more strictly conditioned. The panels thus formed at once become the necessary unit of scale in breaking up the sides. More strictly the unit is an imagined common measure of back-panel and sides. The designer does not, of course, geometrically work this out, but it is the sense of this relation that determines him in the proportion and placing of his masses and details, and a lettered panel limits the design very completely indeed.

Starting from this fact of the panels on the back, the designer may actually carry the lines of the bands across the sides, as in "Grass of Parnassus," or he may not; but he must throughout give to these lines an imaginary extension in placing the design upon the sides, and if he puts a title on the cover, this must be considered in its scale and place together with that on the back.

Many treatments of the covers are possible. Each may be considered as one large panel —" Catalogue of the Arts and Crafts Exhibition," Fig. 122, or broken up in various ways into smaller panels—" Grass of Parnassus," Fig. 120, or both taken together as one panel crossed by the back— "The Golden Hind," Fig. 123. In this last case a design may be thrown across the two covers, but each part must be to some extent self-sufficient, since the whole is rarely seen at one time. In connection with this particular application, it may be added that the treatment of book designs will

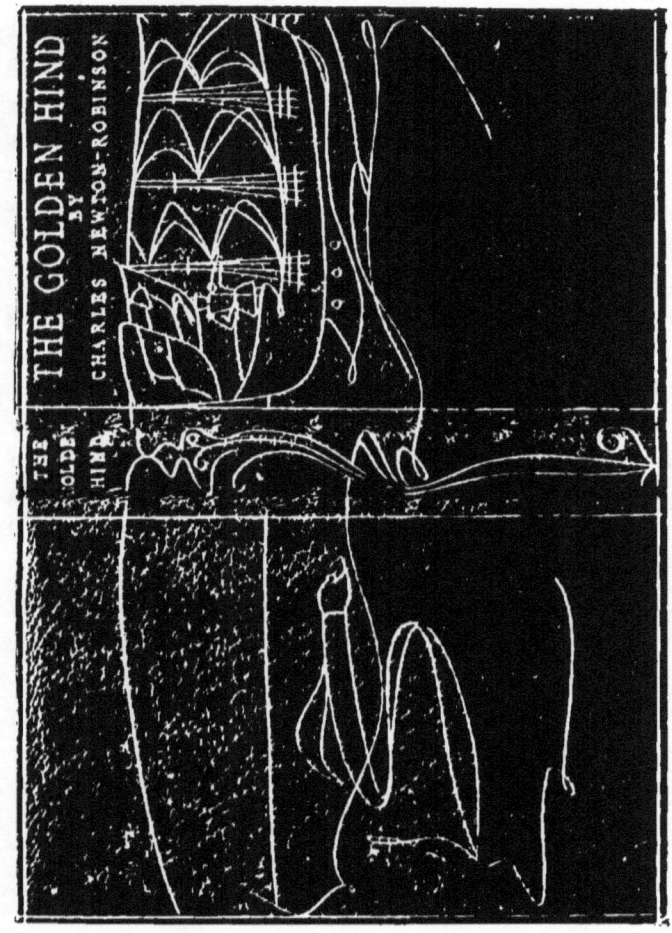

Fig. 123.—MacColl Binding to the Voyage of "The Golden Hind."

differ a good deal according to the way in which a book is regarded—whether as put on a shelf with other books and exposing its back, or laid on a table and exposing its side, or most reasonably, perhaps, as something turned about in the hands.

A favourite plan in designing for book-covers, as for the decoration of the printed page, is to plan a border with a design that runs round. It is a plan seldom satisfactorily carried out, not only from the difficulty of turning the corner — a difficulty more often cut mechanically than solved—but because a design that turns a second corner is almost necessarily broken-backed in effect. An ideal law of growth or motion controls ramified or wave design even when least naturalistic in its forms. A design returning into itself is more satisfactory on a circular plan than on one that is right-angled.

It may be added, in this connection, that when a highly abstract or conventionalised ramification is introduced, a displeasing effect will result from giving those branches naturalistic leaves or flowers. It is for this reason we feel uncomfortable when in certain designs attributed to the Eves, and much imitated, we find little leaves tied on at intervals to a rigid segmental form. It is better to follow in the path of the best Gothic designers, who gave a pillar-tree pillar-leaves that the ingenious have in vain tried to identify with any one plant. So should the book-tree have book-leaves and flowers at an equal remove from nature with its stem."

CHAPTER X

WOMEN WORKERS IN THE ART CRAFTS.

"MAN for the field and woman for the hearth, Man for the sword and for the needle she," requires, so far as the last statement is concerned, a very liberal interpretation, the word "needle" having to symbolise tools in general. For women are doing most excellent work in the Art crafts; so excellent, indeed, that it occurs to me it would be wiser if many who are now trying to win positions as painters and sculptors were to direct their energies and abilities into the less ambitious groove of applied art; success of a quite satisfactory kind might be theirs.

When I was trained as a glass painter, I do not remember any woman who had won a reputation as a painter of church windows, though some few were employed as "tracers." Miss Mary Lowndes, who has a studio at Chelsea, is doing some excellent glass, and I was glad of the opportunity which a visit to her, at Messrs. Britten and Gilson's, where she paints her windows, afforded me of seeing the glass she uses in her work. This make of glass was the suggestion of Mr. Edward Prior. It is dull on one side, and, instead of being rolled or blown, is moulded in

X

small pieces, and varies considerably in thickness, from half-inch to one-eighth. The glass has somewhat the effect that cutting gives a gem, and is exceedingly brilliant; while, at the same time, it cannot be seen through. This thickness

Fig. 124.—Window.   By Mary Lowndes.

gives a window made up of it a substance and quality not obtainable when the ordinary thin glass is employed. It is obvious that glass of great beauty in itself should have as little painting put upon it as possible, for all paint applied to glass tends to destroy its brilliance.

Miss Lowndes, in fact, keeps her painting almost entirely

Fig. 125.—Church of the Holy Innocents, Lamarsh.
By Mary Lowndes.

[Owing to length of block it has had to be divided.]

to the subject portions of her window, and gets much of her effect by the distribution of the leads and the selection and arrangement of the colour. The glass itself is much more costly than the ordinary makes, and the leading of it again is troublesome, so cheap work is not possible. But in a window which, unless accident befalls it, may live through the ages to come, cheapness should surely not be the first consideration. People will willingly give hundreds for a canvas painted by a popular artist, and yet the same folk expect a window, much more costly to produce than a picture, to be made for a few pounds.

Miss Lowndes worked for some little time with Mr. Holi-day at cartoon-making; but as regards the technique of glass painting, she is self-taught. Mr. Christopher Whall has not been without his influence upon Miss Lowndes, and she speaks with the enthusiasm of a pupil about him. Miss Lowndes relies upon her drawings from the model in her cartoons, but as the actual painting of the glass is done by her, the necessity of making elaborate cartoons does not exist. Nothing is left to the glazier but the cutting and leading, as the artist selects each piece of glass used in making a window ; and this ought always to be the case in the flesh and important parts of the drapery. Flesh painting on glass is too often of the most ignorant kind, the work of mechanics with neither feeling nor knowledge to give charm or quality to their work. How many women with a considerable amount of academic knowledge, which comes of good training, might take up glass painting and achieve success, that is denied them in the more am-bitious fields of painting and sculpture ! Some technical training would be necessary, but this would soon be acquired by one with the training of an art student to start with.

Miss Mary Nevill, who works at Edgbaston, Birmingham, is also winning a reputation as a designer of painted glass. From the design reproduced (Fig. 126), Miss Nevill is evidently influenced by Burne-Jones and Morris. We are all conscious or unconscious imitators, for what is more natural than to seek to get into our own work the qualities we admire in others? We must first be level with the knowledge of our time, and then we can march forward into the unknown, where only our perception is our guide. Glass painting owes much to Burne-Jones and Morris, just as they owed much to Madox Browne, but I must say here, as I have said before, that the student's personality must make its way through all influences, as the pupa does through its cocoon, if you would soar into the world of Art. So much Art, especially of a decorative nature, is just now too much a reflection, instead of a lamp shining forth with what strength it may to lighten our darkness. The Birmingham Guild of Handicraft I have elsewhere alluded to, but it is a healthy sign that such a purely manufacturing town as Birmingham is doing something to get a little other influence than the purely commercial into what is being done there in the way of craftsmanship.

There is a growing demand for artistic metal-work. People are no longer satisfied with the stock patterns in gas-fittings, electric-light holders, and lamps, but desire something which is not to be seen in every house in the neighbourhood. Miss Esther Moore, whose studio is at Bedford Park, has turned her attention to applied design, and her electric-light holder (Fig. 127) is a specimen of her work in this direction. The panel in low relief (Fig. 128), one of three for a pianoforte front. has a tender gracefulness suitable to the purpose. Miss Moore has in it given play to her

fancy, and the disposition of curves filling out the panel and supporting the figure are skilfully and pleasantly studied. She roughly models the work in wax, then has it cast in plaster, which is then tooled up and finished: an excellent plan where delicacy is required, as plaster can be carved and brought to a high degree of finish. A mould is then made from the plaster, and a casting taken in silver or bronze.

What a field there is before the student who has had a training in modelling! Instead of waiting for the elderly gentleman to come along, with nicely trimmed whiskers or curling beard (and probably retreating hair), to have his bust modelled, let the student do some original work

Fig. 126.—Window. By Mary Nevill.

in metal, if it be only a lock plate, like that of Miss Florence
Steel's (Fig. 129), and I feel sure there is a world ready to
patronise her. For the last few years excellent metal-work,

Fig. 127. Electric-Light Holder. By Esther M. Moore.

as these pages attest, has been produced in many directions,
and there is a large public capable and ready to patronise
an original worker in metal.

At the Arts and Crafts Exhibitions some good book-binding has been shown, the work of women. As the sewing of books is always done by them, there is no reason why the "forwarding" should be left to men. Leather work would appear to be a craft in which women might do very excellent work.

Fig. 128.—Panel in Bas-relief.
Esther M. Moore.

I am able to give an example of one of Miss Birkenruth's bindings (Fig. 132); and in another chapter may be seen specimens of bindings by Miss MacColl.

Repoussé leather might be more extensively employed on book-covers than it is, for the effects obtainable are rich and not out of place, provided that too much relief is not given to any portion of the design. Some specimens of work of this character of the fifteenth century I have seen show what can be done with repoussé leather when skilful hands are directed by a trained imagination.

The School of Wood-carving has a woman for its manager, and has two assistant teachers—a book-cover by one of them (Fig. 130), Miss M. E Reeks, being given. A great many of the pupils who go to the school for instruction are women, and wood-carving appears to be popular with lady amateurs. Miss M. Hussey, of Salisbury, who has exhibited some quite original carved frames at the Arts and Crafts, has allowed me to reproduce a specimen of her work (Fig. 131). It has the great merit of gaining distinction by its original treatment, which is more than can be said of a good deal of the wood-carving that one sees ; and it is this individuality—I must apologise for having to use the word so often which is such an encouraging sign among the younger craftsmen whose work I have been privileged to inspect during the writing of this book.

Women's work is accused of its want of character and its tendency to pettiness, which comes of smallness of vision. I am not here posing as the superior critic, but I question whether, considering the disadvantages so many women workers in Art labour under, and how much less thorough is the training so many of them receive compared to men, their work is so far below the male standard as some critics infer. I do think, however, that if women are to do themselves justice, they should try to obtain a more thorough training than they are inclined to be content with, for if they take a craft up as the business of their life, they must not fall back upon their sex as an excuse for technical deficiencies. From some experience, I can say that women think too often that a course of lessons is going to enable them to rush full-blown into workers, yet when it comes to it women are more patient, painstaking, and even drudging than men ; and these qualities ought to carry them far in the crafts.

The carving and decorating of frames might receive

much more attention at the hands of craftswomen than has

Fig. 129.— Lock Plate.
Florence Steele.

been the case. Many painters would, I feel sure, be willing to pay for original frames, if they knew where to go for them, instead of putting up with the composition ones which are so generally used. But a woman would have to be prepared to work for a time with some want of patronage until she had won for herself a *clientèle* by the excellence of her craftsmanship and the originality of her designs. From some experience I am led to say that women expect too much at the outset. I have known amateurs who expect in half-a-dozen lessons to become fully equipped to follow a craft, and make a good living out of it; whereas a moment's reflection ought to convince them that much practice, as well as study, goes to the making of a craftsman, and distinction, and with it monetary success, is only won after a considerable output of energy, the exhibition of much

patience, and a considerable belief in one's self. One's
hopes are high, I know, at the outset, and waiting is

Fig. 130.—A Presentation Book-Cover. Designed and Carved by
M. E. Reeks.

weary work ; but I. who have gone through all this, can tell
you that you should only be " baffled to fight harder," nor
" dream that right, though worsted, wrong will triumph."

Then, again, one cannot ignore what is known as the business side of Art, especially in Art that is applied, say, to the furnishing of a house ; and here I fear that women allow themselves to be beaten by an unthinking disregard

Fig. 131.   Carved Frame.   By M. Hussey.

of such small considerations as punctuality, price, and purpose.   It has been said that there is no sentiment in business, and craftswomen would do well to remember this, especially in dealing with firms who only view the crafts as

they would any other commodity. The experience of all
women workers I have spoken to points to this, that,

Fig. 132. — Binding. By Miss Birkenruth.

granting an ordinary School of Art training, it is necessary
to build your craftsmanship upon that in order to acquire

the necessary technique, and during this second probation

Fig. 133.—The Iris Lace Bordering. Designed by Colonel Jemmitt Browne. 7 inches wide.

you must keep a light as well as a stout heart. Those who
have from the outset only trained themselves in the practice

of a particular craft, must remember that if they are only finger machines a corresponding small measure of success is for them : they can never inherit the land that might be theirs were they more fully equipped. Drawing from nature, both from plants and the figure, should run parallel with technical instruction, for you cannot have too varied a training ; and change of work as well as study keeps the mind pliant and fresh, and your hands will do things undreamed of by the mechanic, and astonishing to yourself.

I shall finish this chapter with a word of praise for the excellent way women have organized classes in craftsmanship in country places. This movement, with its small beginnings, is, I believe, the one that will restore Art to our industries and make our people once again cunning workers. The annual exhibition at the Albert Hall of the Home Arts and Industries Association enables us to measure what is being done, and I am glad to be able to give in this book two or three specimens of work wrought under the stimulus of this association.

CHAPTER XI.

SURFACE DECORATION.

N the brief survey we have taken of some of the prominent Art crafts, I have not had occasion to say much about design in the abstract, partly because, as I hold, that design and craftsmanship are inseparable, and partly because design cannot be taught. But it would appear an oversight to ignore altogether Surface Decoration, so this chapter will consist in the main of notes written to accompany some examples of surface decoration I have selected from the pages of *The Art Journal*.

The screen, Fig. 134, by Sir E. Burne-Jones, is a good example of the painter's method as applied to decoration. One can see the influence of glass painting in the way the forms are shaped, as though a lead line had to come around them— indeed, I believe this screen is adapted from a design made originally for glass. The painter of a picture has to study "values" and surfaces as well as how to brush on the colour, but the decorator has to think of every part of his design as an agreeable shape, fitting in each portion with ingenuity and, at the same time, with an eye to the whole effect. The flames, for instance, are not the representation of a particular flash of light, but are evolved from the painter's inner consciousness,

the forms being conditioned to a large extent by the
spaces occupied by them.   The painter deals with repre-

Fig. 134.   Screen.   By Sir E. Burne-Jones.

sentation, the designer with construction; yet there must be
truthfulness so that the work may be convincing, and this
can only come of the study of actual flames, so that the

o

lines of his design may be suggested by the lines actual
flames give—the result of observation. A decoration
should be just as truthful, so far as observation and knowledge goes, as a picture, but it cannot be independent of
all else as the work within a frame can.

Burne-Jones is described by a certain class of critics as
a decorative painter, but the term is a question-begging
phrase at best. How far painting can be carried in an
imitative or deceive the-eye direction is one I shall make no
effort to decide. There are they who hold that all pictures
are merely decorations, and that it is better to make no
attempt at imitating surfaces or objects, seeing that " the
best of these are but shadows."

The decorator is generally called upon to do a good deal
of work for the money expended—to cover a much larger
surface for much less money than the painter of pictures,
and it behoves him, therefore, to study economy of means ;
but this does not excuse bad work—bad, that is, in drawing
and colouring, in adaptation or arrangement. A decoration
should be just as good on its own lines as a picture, whereas
the idea seems to be held that a bad picture may be a good
decoration : the work the art gallery rejects may become
the success of the workshop ; a wholly false belief, of
course.

The shutter, Fig. 135, by Mr. Whistler, is a portion of the
celebrated peacock room decorated for the late Mr. Leyland.
It is a most admirable example of painted decoration because
there is no false attempt made at giving a realistic rendering
of the birds, such as a skilful handler of the brush like
Mr. Whistler could have given, but a constructed design in
which the lines are most skilfully and gracefully placed.

Fig. 135.—Shutter. By J. McNeill Whistler.

Mr. Whistler owes something to his study of Japanese art, as he would be the first to acknowledge, and the student could put himself under no better influence for a while than the best Japanese art. A study of their *Kakemonos*, or hanging wall pictures, is specially to be commended. Their knowledge of plant and animal form is what a constant and faithful study of nature alone can give, and the refinement of their rendering of natural forms, the power of selection, their skill in placing and occupying the space gives Japanese work an uniqueness, which made decoration, a few years

Fig. 136.—Ship Frieze. For Mural Decoration. By M. Watson. (South Kensington Schools.)

ago, take a Japanese turn; and the good that a study of their work would have done English designers was to a great extent nullified by an attempt at copying their work, a proceeding as foolish as it was impossible.

The question of how far surface decoration may be naturalesque depends upon the method of reproduction, and the purpose to which the decoration is to be put as well as the time that can be given to it.

A design to be inlaid would obviously have to be simpler in treatment than if it were to be painted, and then again were the painting on the panel, say of a cabinet, it might be carried much further than if you were decorating, say, a pianoforte top, an excellent specimen of which I remember seeing years ago, by Morris, in which the wood was painted white, and an all-over arrangement of foliage was disposed in quiet, low-toned colours. It has always seemed to me better to be frankly decorative than weakly naturalistic : say the forms emphasised by an outline and complicated foreshortening, and light and shade avoided. Not that there is any necessity why decoration should be outlined, as at one time was the vogue (decorative work *then* always implied an outline), but it is better to do this if by so doing you bring your work within the limits of the price to be paid for it. It should be quite excellent within the limits imposed upon it, whereas if a more subtle or pictorial class of work were attempted the fulfilment might then do no more than suggest how insufficient it is, because the standard set is outside the reach either of the worker or his opportunities. A good piece of simple decoration in which the conditions, whatever they may be, are frankly accepted, is of more value artistically and commercially than an inadequate picture. Apart from these considerations a decoration should possess a certain ingenuity of construction or arrange-ment—design, in other words, which is not demanded of the painter of easel pictures. Not that a picture does not need arrangement, but it is of a less obvious nature than a decoration which has to make much of the main lines of the design, for good decoration should always suggest " the being fitted for a place and subordinated to a pur-pose."

The ship frieze, Fig. 136, is a good instance of what is termed decorative adaptation. The artist does not trespass upon the painter's ground, but is content to find a foothold for himself in another field.

The Japanese have been termed born decorators, though this is another misleading or question - begging phrase. What is meant presumably is that they do not attempt realistic representations of nature, which, to some extent, deceive the eye, as the bunch of grapes in the Greek story which even took in the birds, they were so "real." The lacquered box, Fig. 138, is "decorated" in the best sense. A Jap is very dexterous in pencilling what he sees — witness their plant and bird studies in water-colour — but he is, when he comes to occupy a space, as much concerned with an agreeable disposal

Fig. 137.—Kakemono. Sosen.

of his objects as in rendering the objects themselves. This is well illustrated in Fig. 137, where there is a lot of space left plain, and yet the whole panel satisfies the eye, so skilfully are the monkeys and foliage disposed. A space may be occupied as in this *Kakemono*, or filled or covered, and it is in the former treatment that the Japs excel.

A brush in the hands of a Jap is a most sensitive and

Fig. 138.—Lacquered Box. Middle Period of Korin.

expressive tool. By starting with the tip and putting gradual pressure upon it so that it swells out, a Jap makes it discharge its colour, at the same time putting in a leaf or petal or whatever the object is he is rendering. This power of brush work stands him in excellent stead when it comes to decorating a screen or wall picture, as he is able to work effectively as well as rapidly. The student would do well to get into the way of putting in forms from nature by the use of skilful brush work as a Jap does. Rapid work, which comes of skill and knowledge, is always more admirable than laboured, painstaking effects, and the decorator should cultivate skill in brush work *à la Japonaise.*

A Japanese designer delights in angles, and is most skilful in the disposal of them in a design. The lines taken by the trunk, stems, and sprays have a *nervous* quality about them which escapes analysis, yet they are always suggested by nature. The good a study of Japanese painting would do a student is teaching him what to look for in nature. Half the training of an artist is to the end to teach him *to see,* and this is where the study of other men's work may be so beneficial.

Mr. Heywood Sumner has, one might say, made "sgraffito" his own. It is a method of covering a dark cemented surface with a light one, the design being produced by scraping away the upper surface while wet so as to reveal the under one. It is both a permanent and effective form of outside decoration. A certain simplicity is necessary where all forms have to be rendered with a hard definite outline. The example of "The Adoration of the Magi," Fig. 139, gives a good idea of how and what can be done, the utmost use being made of the means at command, with no foolish attempt to strive for too much, or step outside the limits of the craft. To fit the design to the page the block has had to be cut and the centre portion placed below the two side panels.

In needlework we have two good examples, shown recently at the Exhibition of the Home Arts and Industries Association at the Albert Hall: *Haslemere,* by Mrs. God-

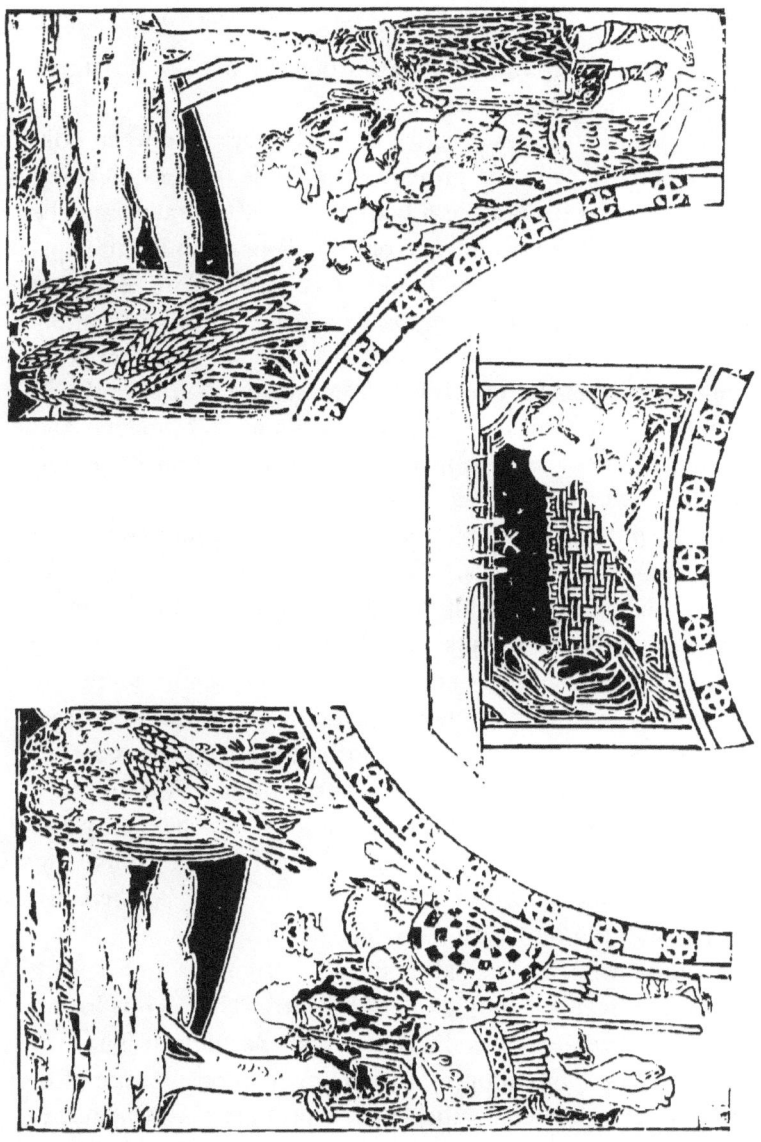

frey Blount, Fig. 140, and the Portière by Messrs. T. Harris & Sons (Fig. 142).

Appliqué is always effective in needlework, and when bold in treatment, as in the present example, is both a quick and telling way of decorating a textile.   Great restraint must be observed by the worker to avoid the disposition of attempting too much instead of frankly recognising and accepting the conditions the craft imposes on one.   This is admirably observed in the example, and at a casual glance appears simple enough to effect, but from some experience I can vouch to the contrary.   To keep one's work elemental and independent of what is merely adventitious requires genius, so rare is it.

The portière was embroidered in flax on linen woven at the Cockermouth Mills.   Flax is a most lustrous material to use with the needle, and for bold work and large designs is to be preferred to silk.   I have seen exhibited at the Donegal Industrial Fund, some excellent embroideries in flax on serge of Keltic design made by the Donegal peasantry in which bold patterns in outline, almost coarsely worked, were employed with considerable effect for such articles as curtains—so much needlework has only the merit of enormous labour to give it value.   It is like the weight of metal making plate valuable, and is, therefore, not doing the best with the craft.

Those who are called upon to design for needlework would do well to study good old work.   The revival in this art some years ago produced an immense output, but little of it will be handed on to a future generation because of its Art value.   I plead guilty, like many another designer, to giving *transcripts* of nature instead of *designs* founded upon

a study of nature, in which an original, skilful. and agreeable
disposition of the main lines of the design was the first consideration. and the clothing of these lines appropriately the
next. There is a long remove between a study of a par-

Fig. 140.—The Purple Ship. Example of Appliqué Tapestry
(Haslemere).

ticular portion of a particular plant and a design founded
upon the same.

A certain severe simplicity should. I think, be seen in
needlework, and I would say that quaintness is to be preferred to naturalness. as the further you get away from the

Fig. 141.— One of the Painted Panels from the Screen in
Ranworth Church, Norfolk.

mere transcript of nature the more you have to depend
upon yourself, and the more chance is there, therefore, of
expressing your individuality. A design is a work of the
imagination as much as a poem or theme in music is, and

Fig. 142. Portière in Harris Line. Embroidered in Flax.

that being so, nature is only the stimulus—the A. B. C. It
is you who have to do the rest; put the A. B. C. into
words, and the words into sentences which shall fall with an
agreeable cadence on the ear and speak at the same time to
the heart.

I am glad to be able to give a sketch (Fig. 141) of one
of the panels in the screen in Ranworth Church, which I
made some few years since when on the Broads. It is an
excellent specimen of decoration, being full of "design."

CHAPTER XII

DECORATION IN RELIEF.

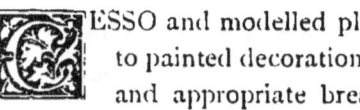ESSO and modelled plaster are very useful adjuncts to painted decoration. All decoration is the skilful and appropriate breaking up of a surface, and modelled work breaks up decoration by giving accent and focussing the interest at certain well-chosen intervals. *Gesso* might be termed modelled painting, for the whitening and glue which really constitutes gesso can be applied to the wood by brushes, for it is to give an *impasto* effect to painted decoration, and not to imitate modelling that gesso should be employed. I remember seeing a grand pianoforte case of painted wood which was decorated with an all-over foliage design painted on in simple tones; some of the leaves and the berries were in gesso, and the effect was most pleasing. The slight accent given to the painted decoration by the portions in relief was of great help to the general effect.

Decoration in modelled plaster occupied a prominent place in the last Arts and Crafts show, and no one has carried this style of work further than Mr. George Frampton, A.R.A. His refined style and originality are shown to great advantage in his work in low relief, whether it be in the silver panels he executed for Mr. Astor, or in the decoration of the frieze in his own drawing-room, which he

Fig. 143.—Portion of Drawing Room designed by George Frampton, A.R.A.

has allowed me to reproduce. He is a great advocate of

Fig. 144.—Sketch Design for proposed Leighton Memorial.
By Geo. Frampton, A.R.A.

painted sculpture provided, he said to me, that the colourist is an artist. Of course in his own work he paints it himself. Certainly some of his tinted plaster panels are quite delightful. They are so fresh in treatment, so emphatic of himself, so removed from any suggestion of manufacture, that it makes them a more than pleasant possession. They are choice, a quality that seems rapidly vanishing in the art work around us, where quantity has taken the place of quality, a large output being a manufacturer's desideratum. Mr. Frampton does not always want to thrust his knowledge of the figure before the public. A modelled frieze I greatly admired consisted of a constructed arrangement of the seeds of the plant Honesty set at regular intervals, and tinted in simple light tones of green, and he pays as much attention to designing and modelling this Honesty as he would to a figure, studying the plant from nature for himself. As a matter of fact I saw the very spray of dried seed vessels in his atelier from which he built up his design.

What keeps Mr. Frampton's work so fresh is that he is always going to the fountain-head, nature. At my request he allowed me to reproduce three of his studies from the model which he made for some of his work in low relief. The two fitted into architectural panels were designed for a bank in Scotland, and were afterwards carved on a large scale in freestone. Considerable skill is shown in the way the figures are accommodated to the eccentric-shaped space which they had to occupy. The seated figure is a study for one of the silver panels before referred to. The figures are drawn from the nude, and the drapery is studied apart and the figures are then clothed. This gives the finished work a sharpness and virility which is to art what the breath of life

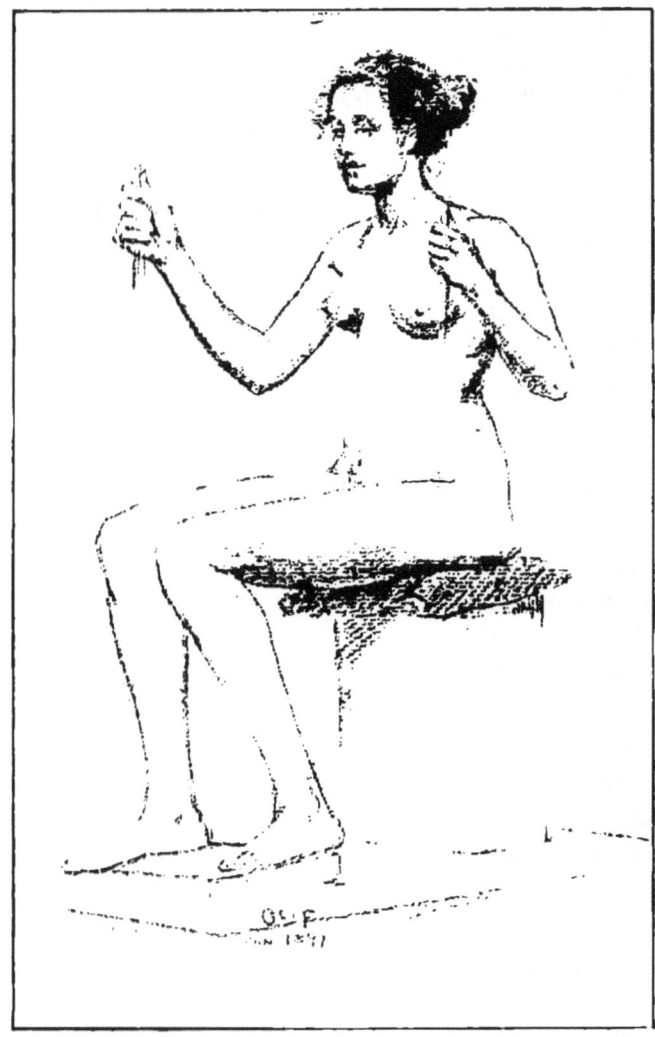

Fig. 145.— Life Study for One of a Series of Small Panels in Low
Relief, Cast in Silver.   By Geo. Frampton, A.R.A.

Fig. 146.   Life Study for Decoration in Low Relief of an Over Door.
By Geo. Frampton, A.R.A.

Fig. 147.   Life Study for Decoration in Low Relief of an Over Door.
By Geo. Frampton, A.R.A.

is to man. The usual figure work in relief offered to the public as decoration by "firms" who do this sort of thing rarely rises above the level of the plaster cornices in a suburban villa. Why don't manufacturers try to get good originals? No one would then blame them for reproducing an unlimited number of a good work, for the multiplication of a thing does not necessarily lessen its art worth. Any reasonable price should be paid for the original, as the cost when spread over thousands of reproductions is hardly worth consideration.

I am glad to be able to give a sketch in clay of another of Mr. Frampton's "Decorations" in relief, the proposed Leighton memorial. As a design it follows exactly the same laws as any other work of art. You have the "lumps" of dark and the "masses" of light, with here and there small ascents, but, looked at with half-closed eyes, the memorial might be a masterly black-and-white study, so broad in treatment is it. The darks, instead of breaking up the lights all over the design, are concentrated in masses, so that the simple rule of keeping the darks out of the lights and lights out of the darks is obeyed.

CHAPTER XIII

WALL-PAPER AND TEXTILE DESIGNING.

THE student who elects to design for wall-papers and textiles must acquire the technique of manufacture, for *how* the design is reproduced tells us to a great extent *how* the designer has to set about his part of the business : his design is conditioned by the method of reproduction, and his labour will be thrown away if he pay insufficient heed to such technical matters.

In a wall-paper the design has to repeat itself in two ways. It must be continuous, so that a constantly revolving cylinder (if it be machine-printed) produces the design, and it must be so arranged as to repeat itself when the pieces are hung side by side. The "repeat," therefore, is of the first importance, and as there are several ways of effecting this some special instruction is necessary, and I should say some practical tuition under a designer the best means of acquiring the *techne*. Schools of Art are supposed to give this instruction, and at some of the large ones, such as South Kensington, the teaching is, I daresay, fairly efficient now, though a few years ago this certainly could not be said. In those days the authorities appeared

Fig. 148. The Inchkeith Wall-Paper. Designed by E. A. Hunter.
Messrs. W. Woollams & Co.

This design might be analyzed as a conceit in the structural lines
with fillings of conventionalised lilies. It is certainly skilfully planned,
and though its "repeat" is emphatic, it would, on a large surface, be a
decorative wall covering.

Fig. 149.—Wall-Paper, by Jeffrey & Co.   Designed by W. Crane.

This is a familiar example of Mr. Crane's decorative adaptation of natural forms to such productions as a wall-paper.   The difficulty here is chiefly in getting the " lines " of the design to flow agreeably, so that when repeated it shall cover the wall of a room pleasantly, without worrying the eye.   As to how naturalesque a paper should be is a question not of rule, but taste.   There are they who dogmatise in this matter, because they want to force their own views upon the world. Let them.   A paper-stainer has to cater for the world, and is generally free of bias.

to have the utterly mistaken idea that design itself could be taught, and there was a period when a certain kind of floral conventionality was looked upon as *the* way. It consisted to a great extent in drawing the plant symmetrically and planning it geometrically, but as for develop'ng the originality of the student, nothing further was from the minds of the authorities. Happily, owing to the pressure from outside, a better system now obtains, and in the judging of works sent in for competition a great advance has been made, for practical men with a recognised position in the crafts are called in to award the prizes, and so a much higher standard has been set. It might be thought that, as wall-papers are " manufactured," the opportunity of expressing your ego is small, and yet originality is the one thing necessary and the only quality that will gain you attention. The personality of some designers in this field is very marked, and the result is their designs have true " s'yle." Some few, perhaps, err in the direction of eccentricity; but I am prepared to forgive originality much, though I fear the manufacturer is not so sympathetic. He has to look at what sells, and his practical knowledge should be worth a good deal to a designer. He should be the designer's " editor," as it were, and most literary men are none the worse for being edited. The tyro, however, is a conceited person, and looks upon himself as allsufficient, and kicks against this editing until hard experience herself edits *him*.

All the large firms are ever on the look-out for originality, and a student who possesses this quality need not be afraid of submitting his views to any of them. If there is anything in them he will quickly be encouraged, and any

Fig. 150.   The Brienne Wall-Paper.   Designed by E. A. Hunter.
Messrs. W. Woollams & Co.

In the " Inchkeith " design the pattern resolved itself into emphatic
structural lines, which were pure ornament and decorative floral fittings.
Here the design is what is termed an all-over pattern, the " repeat "
being to a large extent hidden, so that the surface is broken up
agreeably, and though the design would, when hung, form diagonal
lines, the planning of the pattern is homogeneous, no opposing motif
being introduced.   I should call it, too, a well-drawn design, the artist
exhibiting a nice appreciation of shapes and curves.

technical deficiencies in his designs will be pointed out to him, so that he will quickly drop into the groove.

While writing this I had a chat with the managing

Fig. 151. The Westmeath Wall-Paper. Designed by G. C. Haité, R.B.A., for Messrs. W. Woollams & Co.

designer of one of our best known firms, and he tells me that designs of a very marked character—the most distinctly original ones, in fact—are found not to sell so well as those one is more or less accustomed to, partly because people are like sheep and follow one another, and therefore dread innovation, and partly because these strikingly original wall-papers seem to upset the balance of the room and make ordinary furniture look terribly commonplace. The student, therefore, may take warning from this and keep within recognised boundaries, and be not too original, but just original enough, until he become a force and gain a following ; then he can compel attention and so secure patronage.

I can remember how thrown back I was when I started on my own account, at having my work refused all round, but the fact is it takes one some time to view one's work critically, which is what the buyer you submit it to does. The tyro is blindly hopeful, and rates himself altogether too high. What you think strikingly original is probably the commonplace of the craft you are working for. The student who will trouble to master the technique of wall-paper designing, which may be summarised as, how the design is to repeat, the lines the design makes when seen *en masse* on the walls (this is very important, as many an otherwise good design forms ugly lines or spots when hung), and how many colours it is necessary to use to print it.

Use as few colours as possible is a good general rule, for as each colour requires a separate printing it adds to the cost of the paper to introduce many colours. A clever designer can get all the variety he wants with about four colours, and it would astonish a beginner to see what can be done with *one* colour.

Designing for Textiles is subject to much the same conditions as wall-papers. In fact, many wall-paper designs are adapted to Textiles by the designer himself. The special conditions the work imposes upon you must be observed, and it is necessary, therefore, to find out what these are before bestowing your labour there.

The beginner is apt to be discouraged by the want of

Fig. 152. The Westminster Wall-Paper and Frieze. Designed by Mr. A. Silver, for Messrs. W. Woollams & Co.

patronage at the outset. He makes a design, and is inclined to overrate its merits because of the interest he has taken in it and the trouble it has given him; but I may remind such an one that the firm to whom he submits his effort have brought to them many dozens of designs every

month, and out of this number there must be some of more
than ordinary merit, while yours may not be of that number.
The doors of success open but in very rare instances at the
first knock. You must have the courage which comes of

Fig. 153.—The " Rosebery " Wall-Paper. Designed by Mr. C. F. A.
Voysey, for Messrs. W. Woollams & Co.

belief in yourself to keep on in spite of the want of
encouragement at the outset. Be yourself; put yourself
wholly into what you do; for nothing is more likely to
obtain for you the patronage you desire than an original

Fig. 154.—The "Tewkesbury" Wall-Paper. Designed by Mr. W. V.
Aspen, for Messrs. W. Woollams & Co.

"note." Yet at the outset the chances are you will be a
reflection of the work around you, or of some one craftsman whose ego holds you, and it is not until you have

worked for some time that you will begin to speak in your own language.

Fig. 155.   Prize Design for Wall-Paper.   By P. Shepherd.
(South Kensington Schools.)

A wall-paper design seems to divide itself into two parts. There is the ornamental constructive part of the design (the scaffolding, as it were, of the edifice), *the* important feature. in fact, and the one to which the first and chief attention

Fig. 156. Wall-Paper Design. By C. F. A. Voysey.
(Messrs. Essex & Co.)

must be paid, as the "line" this makes must be studied, so that it will repeat itself agreeably. The filling out of these

Q

constructive lines is a far simpler affair, and should only be considered after they are satisfactorily placed upon the paper.

A knowledge of plant form is essential, and, indeed, the designer should always be on the look-out and try and look at nature as though she were a series of wall-papers, for this idea of making designs should be at the "back of the head" of all students who are bending their talent in this direction. The drawing of plant form should, therefore, be done deliberately towards this end of *making designs*. This amount of subjectiveness on the part of the student is necessary, because he will then more likely seize upon those features in the plant which are ornamental and suggest new combinations, than if he merely sat down and sketched any plant which came across him.

All designs one may say are at least suggested by plant form, if not founded upon some one or more particular plants, for the more abstract a design is, that is, the further it is removed from the particular, and only the principles of plant growth observed, and not the peculiarities of some *one* plant. the more ornamental it becomes.

Let me here again remind you that a design is not necessarily the conventional rendering of plants, the simplifying and adapting of them to a particular purpose, but a combination of lines and forms agreeably disposed and suitably arranged for a particular purpose. The natural form, whether it be a plant, insect's wing, feather, frost on a window pane, flame of a candle, wave of the sea, which gives the suggestion. is not the *end*, but the *means*. You are *designing*, which implies, I take it, that by a pure effort of the mind you are evolving shapes from your inner con-

Fig. 157. Mimosa Filling and Bullfinch Frieze.
By A. J. Baker. Essex & Co.)

Fig. 158.   Wall-Paper Design.   By C. F. A. Voysey.   (Essex & Co.)

The introduction of such emphatic forms like birds in a wall-paper requires to be done with great discrimination and judgment.   There is a tendency to get them very naturalistic; but this Mr. Voysey has avoided, and the birds thus become an integral part of the general scheme.

sciousness and not drawing things already existing, though in carrying out the idea at the back of your head you use forms of things existing just as a writer uses the letters of the alphabet.

William Morris, who gave wall-paper and textile designing a fresh impetus, kept fairly close to nature, that is, you could see often what was the particular plant he had drawn before making his designs. He owed much to Rossetti, who in the backgrounds to his pictures had a happy way of introducing plants, treated not so much in a realistic as a decorative manner. I remember in one picture the painter introduced an *espalier* apple-tree in what we now should call a " wall-paper " manner, though it was Rossetti's manner of drawing the apple-tree that made it " wall-papery."

Morris, it is said, owed much to Gerarde's " Herbal." The illustrations in this fine work are woodcuts of the seventeenth century, and the plants are drawn in a very simple way, so that the growth is shown in much the same way as is seen in a pressed specimen. I can quite think it likely that Morris did find these woodcuts of English plants very useful, for they were already ornamented to some extent in Gerarde, and all he had to do was to interpret them in his own way and for the purpose he required them.

Think of line and mass before all else, and I have found that a big brush and colour is a better way to rough out a design, after the few preliminary charcoal markings, than any other medium. A brush is so pliant, and you can get a sweep so much more fluently than with a stiff, inflexible point. By using a brush and colour you are more likely to get " breadth " into your work than you are by the use of a point, which is apt to induce niggle and littleness. You

work with freedom, too, and can soon alter and blot out
with Chinese white, and this is very important in blocking

Fig. 156.—Cretonne, by Wardle & Co.   Designed by S. G. Mawson.

out a design, for you work then at high pressure, and want
a medium, therefore, that is quickly expressive.   When the
design has been knocked about and studied from every

Fig. 160.—Cactus Frieze. 21 inches wide.

Designed by Arthur Gwatkin. Produced by Wyle & Lockhead, Ltd.

point of view, then you can make a careful tracing of it and transfer it to a clean sheet of paper, so that when it comes to drawing it in carefully you can do it with certainty. This method of tracing is useful in this way, that in going over your own work a second time you refine it and leave out what is redundant; you pare it down to its elements, and so bring about that simplicity which is the foundation of all good art.

It may be worth your while to make a tracing from your tracing, and still further refine it. But before you finally colour it be sure that the design repeats agreeably, and does not fall into disagreeable lines or spots, for many a good idea is spoilt as a wall-paper by repeating in an ugly manner.

The few examples of papers given must not be considered representative: they were to hand, and so far are useful to the student as showing him what some few designers are doing. A whole book might be devoted to this one branch of art, but my object in this work is to take a general survey of craftsmanship.

I may just say that the work of Mr. Voysey and Mr. Gwatkin in wall-paper designing is strong in the ego of these two craftsmen. The former's severe restrained style is seen in Figs. 156 and 158, while the very bold ornamental frieze, Fig. 160, by Mr. Gwatkin is a very admirable example of the adaptation of plant form to design. In Mr. Baker's mimosa filling, Fig. 157, nature is more closely followed, the skill being shown in the play of curve and distribution of the masses.

CHAPTER XIV.

THE CRAFTSMAN UP-TO-DATE AND HIS OUTLOOK.

> " Others mistrust and say, " But time escapes :
>   Live now or never ! "
> He said, " What's time ? leave Now for dogs and apes !
>   Man has For ever."—*A Grammarian's Funeral.*

HERE are periods in the world's history when progress is very slow, and the man who desires to push ahead grows impatient, and then hopeless, at the stagnation around him ; the time seems not with him, and he is left to eat his heart out with neglect. These periods are very deadening to the craftsman, as I realise when I look back twenty years. But I can also tell my readers that the world, out of joint as it may seem to the youthful enthusiast now, doesn't want as much setting right as it did when I was serving an apprenticeship in the crafts. The amount of public recognition given to an original worker now is greater than anything dreamed of in my apprentice days, and it shows me that the world has moved on quickly since then, and progress, measured both by results and time, has been as rapid as before it was slow.

It is agreed on all hands that the art of the early Victorian days had reached a very low ebb. It ran in the same groove—"the same old rut would deepen year by year." Personality, originality, were wanting. The crafts were followed in a machine-like way, and a dead level of mediocrity was reached that astounds us when we look back forty years. Recognition was given to the firm, never to the individual. People bought certain things because a shopkeeper sold them. None asked themselves why. The age was mechanical, and folk lived mechanically because they did not think. A craftsman now, with any skill and personality, stands a good chance of a hearing, and as much (if not more) attention is given to the crafts as to pictures and statuary. We realise that what surrounds us on every hand should be interesting, the work of an original mind instead of the output of machines. The craftsman has come into his heritage. The land is his to possess if he will.

This happier and lovelier state has been brought about by here and there the man of strong personality, through good and evil report, in spite of neglect and the "ignorance of office," lifting up his voice and showing that he would not let circumstances crush him. In the slavery of convention in which the craftsman in the old days was brought up he might easily have had his ego crushed out of him, but he persisted in expressing himself in his own way, and would not allow his voice to be drowned in the jargon of his time.

All new impulses have to stand the test of ridicule. They have to outlive the opposition of the ignorant and the sneers of the prejudiced. One remembers the first exhibition of the " Arts and Crafts," and what a source of merriment it

was to those who had not the eyes to see the new order of
things. Of course in all new movements there are excres-
cences which time has to wear away : a tendency towards
exaggeration and the setting up of the eccentric and bizarre
to supplant the commonplace. The humourist is right
in fastening upon these and laughing them out of existence.
That which is permanent in the movement will be all the
better for the bracing it receives by this criticism, unkind
and unjust as it may seem to a few enthusiasts to whom
ridicule is so paralyzing. But no really good thing was
ever laughed out of the world. " Though much is taken,
much abides," and that which time leaves us is of real
worth. The world does not willingly let go cunning
work.

The Arts and Crafts Exhibitions were the outcome of the
Art Workers' Guild, and this solidarity of interests which
this Guild symbolizes has given a great impetus to craftsmanship. Some of the older workers have thought that the
" Arts and Crafts " are narrow in their sympathies, and only
bring to the front the work of a particular school. Certainly some ungenerosity of treatment has been meted out
to a few well-known craftsmen, and one professional wood-
carver told me that the committee seemed to him to prefer
the " rabbit-hutch " school (as he termed the somewhat
unskilful wood-work shown) to the technical skill of highly
trained wood-carvers. The society would not, I imagine,
deny that they, in their selection and rejection, have not
shown impartiality. Absolute justice doesn't exist, and the
critics of the " Arts and Crafts " should remember that in
bringing before the public certain work which seems to
them of good report they may have turned away work

excellent in every way, but wanting, perhaps, this personal quality, which is another word for originality. When you turn aside from the work you find around you to search for that which is the outcome of other impulses, it must appear to those minds which have become hardened by habit and therefore disinclined to take in new ideas that eccentricity rather than real merit obtains recognition, to the exclusion of the work to which we have grown more or less accustomed. Any distinctly new departure will beget the disapprobation of the average man, and that is why the work of some of the world's geniuses has, when it first appeared, had nothing but scorn and ridicule hurled at it.

On the other hand, I sympathize with the older worker whose labours receive no recognition at the hands of the new society, and that because it lacks a certain up-to-dateness or modernity. " Man should delight in his work, for that is his portion," and a society which exists to submit craftsmanship to the world cannot be too broad in their sympathies. It should be ready to see the merit in all work which is done lovingly and skilfully. The way the thing is done, finger dexterity, hand cunning, the triumph of mind over matter—whatever you choose to call it, does and should appeal to man, who is " a tool-using animal." The public is the only critic, after all, whose verdict is of any practical use ; and I think that the less a society assumes the function of critic towards the work sent for display the better. Who is to judge what is of good report? We all know what is termed manufacture—work that takes the eye and has its price, which is the outcome of a machine (human though it may be), and not that of the earnest worker who puts himself into his work. Such we can and should exclude; but when it is a question of judgment as to the position of a particular work in Art, then I think we should remember Kipling's dictum that there are *nine and sixty ways*, and that the one which appeals to us is after all only *one*.

Throughout this book it has seemed no part of my duty to offer criticism on the illustrations. The fact that I have selected them implies that in some way or the other they help the subject in hand by illustrating some phase of craftsmanship. That I have my preferences I will not deny, but there is no necessity why I should put them down in writing unless my subject would be helped thereby, and I cannot see that it would. I would have included other examples had it been possible, but the pages were filled and I had to stop, not because I was wholly satisfied with all that are here, but because in this practical world you have to do your "best at a venture," and not wait for perfection.

The Arts and Crafts Exhibitions ought to mark progress, and should be thoroughly representative of all the virile work of the day. They have done immense good, because these shows educate the public and make them interested in craftsmanship. One solicitor friend when he came to furnish his house, tried, as far as was possible, to have things made for him. He desired to be brought into contact with the worker instead of going to some big emporium. Think how much more valuable, because of their personality, our surroundings would be to us if they vividly brought before us the egos of so many workers instead of No. So-and-so in the pages of a store catalogue! Human association, I

take it, is what makes everything in this world interesting
to man, seeing that man is his chiefest study, and therefore
what man produces has some likeness of himself in it.
Those who are in the fortunate position of being able to
spend money on the furnishing of their houses should look
upon it as a privilege which their wealth gives them of being
able to seek out cunning workers to supply them with their
necessities, and so build up an environment which "use
cannot wither nor custom stale." I have said elsewhere,
and I repeat here, that great responsibility rests with the
patron, for he can greatly help the worker by discriminating
praise and patronage. I believe Ruskin says somewhere
that there is more genius in spending money wisely than in
getting it.

The craftsman must be practical, and not drive patronage
from him either by his obstinacy in refusing to heed the
wishes of his client, or by being regardless of his pocket.
Possible patrons are frightened off by the idea that work is
going to be so much more costly if he search out for a
worker himself than if he go to a shop for the article. The
craftsman must fix no false standard of price, but be prepared to do a fair day's work for a fair day's pay. He
must not think of, here and there, the artist raking in his
thousands a year by painting commonplace people in a
commonplace way, but of the rank and file, the average
worker's guerdon. Were he a clerk he could tell by the
law of average what his income is likely to be. Why,
therefore, because he is a craftsman, should he not be prepared to strike an average and go in for the "living wage"?
There is a "joy in the working" which transcends all other
payment; and so long as one can enjoy such comfort as

is necessary to do one's work in, little more should be expected.

There is a great field before the worker in the crafts now, and if he will only gather his harvest in the right way he will not have to remain idle ; but he must not look upon himself as a specially gifted individual upon whom wealth ought to be showered, but as an art worker who, in return for being allowed to live in reasonable comfort, such as the society around him enjoys, is prepared to give the world of his best, and so make his work a joy to himself and to his patrons. To use Ibsen's luminous phrase : "He must bring himself into harmony with the attainable."

When Keats wrote "Beauty is truth, truth beauty," he was probably thinking of some Grecian urn or other beautiful product of man's skill, and he felt that beauty in work is the result of love and reverence—truth, as he termed it. It comes of a belief in ourselves which makes us put ourselves vehemently into what we do. This gives work strength. We must labour patiently, diligently, lovingly, and to do this implies reverence. We do not love a liar or a deceitful person, and we cannot reverence work that is a pretence. If we expand what Keats meant by truth we see that it can be split into love and reverence, and still further subdivided were we on a metaphysical quest. Plato expands goodness into beauty, symmetry, and truth.

Beauty *is* truth. Beauty being a moral quality, we can understand that untruthfulness is opposed to it. We cannot love a person who lies to us. He has lost moral beauty. Why a tradesman's wares are wanting in beauty is that we see no love in their production, " no tricks of the tools' true play," no striving of a soul for utterance, but so much weight of work for so much weight of money. They are too largely a sham, an affectation and pretence, wanting in truth and therefore in beauty. But even " the firm " is forced by the growing interest taken in craftsmanship to move on ; so now we have " art fabrics," " art papers," " art furniture." The æsthetes were laughed at in " Punch " some years ago: now we see that it is to a tradesman's advantage to tack " Art " on to his business. We have moved on a good deal these last twelve years, and we ought to make still more progress if our craftsmen are true to themselves and avoid " fashion,"—the pandering to a mere whim.

All artists, whatever be the medium in which they work, experience disappointment at the outset, and invariably have their efforts refused all round. It is the experience of most of the *now* successful writers, and so it is of craftsmen when passing from the state of pupilage into that of workers. Always have a clear outlook on life, and therefore I put these warnings here, so that the student may, like a good mariner in stormy weather, keep a sharp look-out. I remember when I started working on my own account how I would go out in the morning with my wares (whatever they happened to be) under my arm, filled with an ambition quite high enough to overleap itself, apart from the value, or the want of it, of my wares. Not only was everything possible, but probable too ! A few hours among the firms I offered the output of my brains to sent me back dejected and disheartened. I went out an optimist; I returned a pessimist : for a while the sun had set in the heavens. But that utterly cast-down attitude passes away, and you return to the fight with more staying power each time you receive a repulse.   How cheered I was when I read for the first time those noble lines of Browning :

> "Never one who turned his back but marched breast forward,
>   Never doubted clouds would break ;
>   Never dreamed though right were worsted, wrong would triumph,
>   Held we fall to rise, are baffled to fight harder,
>   Sleep to wake."

After a time, if you don't "welcome each rebuff," you are not surprised at receiving them, because you are on the look out for failure and are prepared to have your work returned on your hands.   When it does find a home, then is the moment supreme.   To feel that you have the privilege of speaking your mind to the world—for you can do that in a wall-paper or a finger-plate as much as in a story—is a privilege worth going through a good deal to obtain.

Have an infinite belief in possibility, but be prepared for failure, for it must come to every one some time or other. As Cromwell is reported to have said, " Trust in God, but keep your powder dry."

Many an earnest worker, in the solitude of his atelier, grows dismayed at times because he does not "get on," and sees charlatanism preferred to honesty.   The short cut to success (whether you mean artistic or mercantile) doesn't pay.   Truth must be the foundation upon which a crafts- man has to build.   He must work out all that is in him, and, so far as the exigencies of life will allow, be faithful to his highest aspirations, for his " reach will always exceed his grasp" under the most favourable conditions.   He must go on working quietly, doing what comes to him with the utmost of his power, leaving the future to take care of itself, for happily it is hidden from him.   I wish such simple counsel had been put before me at the outset of my career. It would have saved me much loss of time later on.   Good work tells in the long run, quicker than the beginner is apt to imagine.   Keats, when he said a thing of beauty is a joy for ever, might have also said that there is always *one* eye at least on the look out for it ; and therefore to throw yourself fully into all you do is the surest way to reach, what every worker requires, recognition.   You are apt to think that your voice is drowned by the noise of the crowd, and that to make yourself heard you must mount the tub and thump the drum.   Is it not the still small voice that governs our actions potent before all else ?

I don't wish this to be a " counsel of perfection," but the experience of a worker after twenty years placed at the disposal of those who are coming after.

There are no divine tips the knowledge of which will enable you to push ahead quickly, and those who profess to have discovered them you may take for charlatans.   Art admits of no rules : it refuses to be circumscribed by such arbitrary bonds.   Bacon said truly art is accomplished by a happy felicity and not by rule, and the so-called canons of art are not to be found except by pedants on the prowl.

Knowledge is gained by observation and reflection, and each worker has to make his own rules.   I remember how, years ago, when I consulted what were considered *the* text-books on design, how entirely I was led away from the proper study by their aphorisms and canons and principles. These guides obscured one's sight and took one off terra firma, to leave one floating in nebulosity as unsatisfactory as it was unsubstantial.   The amount of time, too, one wastes in studying the art of various epochs and peoples !   Theory is developed out of practice, and should not be thrust so entirely to the front as has been the case, any more than is grammar in the modern method of teaching a foreign language.

And remember, too, that all these aids are only means, not the end. In all questions relating to æsthetics much must escape analysis. The true artist, as Ruskin has reminded us, knows less about method than anyone; how he does it is a matter he has never inquired into, and when Reynolds did inquire into it he got no further (if as far) than the most mediocre dauber might have done. Still, what is called "shop," the comparing of notes among workers, is useful as it is pleasant; only one must not take the further step which leads to making what are pious opinions or views absolute; fixed beliefs necessary to artistic salvation. I have endeavoured to avoid dogmatism in this work, and I can only hope I have succeeded.

You must always remember, too, that in all your studies, whether from life or what other masters have done, it is left to you to show us what *you* can do; and what the world demands of you is that you put yourself wholly into all you do. Could the contemplation of the work around us, whether new or old, the studying of so-called text-books, and the knowledge of the "principles" they are supposed to inculcate make artists of us, how many masters there would be! But all these aids are only of use to the student who has an artistic ego, for when you come to make an original effort the mind has to be cleared of these principles before it begins to work. In writing, for instance, one would never get a sentence down if one had nothing but grammar and syntax before one's eyes.

In all really good work there is a quality which is personal to the author and which cannot be reduced to a principle, for it escapes analysis ; just as in mediocre work it is the absence of "*that*," as some one termed the quality which makes a work live.   One only learns by the practice of one's calling, and those moments of inspiration when one is lifted up quite above one's ordinary level for the while to soar in the empyrean, come oftenest to him who gives the strictest attention to his business.   Don't wait for these moments ; work on in all sincerity and they will visit you like angels unawares.

The one idea I have strenuously brought forward in this work is the necessity for originality.   All art work seems to me an excuse for the expression of your ego, and this is developed by the practice of your calling.   The student may be conscious that he lacks ideas and doesn't feel that he has much to say, but before that question can be decided I would remind him that ideas develop as one obtains a firmer grip over one's work.   I have found in my own experience that you may start with a meagre idea, and in pursuing it other ideas are evolved, often of more worth than the initiatory one.   No man can gauge his capacity ; it is an unknown quantity.   Some great men have been dunces, apparently, at school, but this was only apparent, simply because they had not then been caught up into the frenzy of the work that was to make them famous.   Those who score in schools, whether of art or otherwise, and gain prizes and medals, are not always those who go from strength to strength.   Many plants will flower profusely and yet not fruit well.

Do not easily be discouraged.   There are many diffi-.

culties to be surmounted, however lowly your aims may be, but the artist lives, I take it, to triumph over material. It is what the world enjoys in all artistic productions—man's power to shape his thoughts by compelling the material, whatever it be he works in, to obey; as Abt Vogler said of his art, "bidding my organ obey, calling the keys to their work," and to quote again from this stimulating poem of Browning's:

"And God has a few of us whom He whispers in the ear;
The rest may reason and welcome, 'tis we musicians know."

SCHOOLS OF ART AND PLACES OF TUITION.

The schools of art in the various important towns, drawing their inspiration from the central institution at South Kensington, are the most accessible places throughout the country where some sort of art tuition may be obtained. "The South Kensington System" has been severely criticised and largely condemned by some writers for its inefficiency and the misdirection of the student, and has been charged with being a deadening influence, owing to a hard-and-fast administration of a cast-iron system. Such a criticism as this last is true to a great extent of all systems. We must remember that the South Kensington system was a creation in the first instance, a laudable attempt to give some art training to our *ouvriers*. A school of art, in any true sense, is a growth starting from a strong central individuality, attracting the more imitative natures around it to carry on the influences emanating from the initiatory mind. South Kensington was to art very much what a paper constitution is to a people, and it is not until both have been well buffeted about and almost pulled to pieces that the good in them is apparent. South Kensington, as a late national scholar told me, has never professed *to teach design*, only to give *training in drawing*. What it has done to encourage art as applied to manufactures is to offer prizes for designs of various works, such as metal and wall-papers, and in these pages will be found a few reproductions of some of these prize designs. What the severest critic can truthfully say is, that either from without or within South Kensington has advanced with the times, and, looking back as I can upon what it was twenty-three years ago, I can mark the advance made all round. The earnest student rises superior to the most adverse conditions; for the lazy scholar may gain no benefit from a good school, while the worker, while he will gain enormously by good tuition, will not be utterly thwarted by inefficient or bad. The fact that the later judges at these annual competitions have been men from without, of the standing of the late William Morris, is positive evidence that South Kensington has moved on.

One grows tolerant with time, and I, who ten years ago would have been a wholly adverse critic of South Kensington and its ways, am conscious that it is easier to condemn an institution trying to do something to leaven the lump of solid ignorance than to set up anything better to take its place; and I would therefore do what little lays in my power to make it a more potent influence for good than it is than advocate the root-and-branch cure.

Some of the large towns have developed excellent schools, and I can point to no more flourishing one than that at Birmingham, where most excellent work is turned out. A desire to get clean away from the art of the manufacturer is the healthiest sign about this Birmingham guild of handicraft.

" The Central School of Arts and Crafts " founded by the London County Council has its ateliers at 316, Regent Street, opposite the old Polytechnic. The Directors are George Frampton, A.R.A., and W. R. Lethaby. A staff of teachers in the various crafts is engaged; among them I may mention Mr. Christopher Whall for stained glass, and Mr. Alexander Fisher for enamelling. This is quite a new institution, and I can do no more than call attention to it.

At the old West London School of Art, in Great Titchfield Street, technical classes are held in wood carving, brick and stone carving, and other subjects, under the patronage of the Carpenters' Company.

The School of Art Wood-Carving has shifted from the Albert Hall to the Central Technical College, Exhibition Road, South Kensington. Instruction is given to both professional and amateur students.

The City and Guilds South London Art Schools are at 122 and 124, Kennington Park Road, S.E., and also at Finsbury. Technical instruction under various masters in the art crafts is given, as well as in drawing and modelling.

At several of the schools of art special attention is given to certain of the art crafts. At Lambeth, for instance, many of Messrs. Doulton's pottery painters were, I know, at one time drawn from the local school of art. At Chiswick, again, the art crafts receive much attention. Mr. Catterson Smith told me that he received his pre-liminary training in metal work there.

At Es-ex House, Mile End Road, Mr. Ashbee organizes classes through the winter in woodwork and metal ham-mering.

The Royal School of Art Needlework is in Exhibition Road, South Kensington. Instruction can be obtained by female students for certain fees.

The Royal Female School of Art, 43, Queen's Square, Bloomsbury. The training here is on similar lines to that at South Kensington, but I believe special attention is paid to obtaining an outlet for the workers ; chromolithography, I believe, being a speciality with them.

The Art Workers' Guild holds its meetings in the hall at Clifford's Inn, E.C. Papers are read on pertinent subjects by various members, and a discussion follows. Membership is obtained by nomination and election, but the applicant must be a bona-fide worker, though he may be a painter or a craftsman or sculptor.

The triennial exhibitions of the Arts and Crafts Society have hitherto been held at the New Gallery in the autumn. This society is not connected with the guild, but many members belong to both. It is a most interesting résumé of the work of each three years, and these shows have done much to stimulate public interest in craftsmanship.

The Home Arts and Industries Association, for the revival and encouragement of the art crafts in villages, hold their annual exhibition of such of the work executed during the past year each summer at the Albert Hall. This is another show that "marks time," and very encouraging have the results been so far.

The Clergy and Artists' Association, 6, Victoria Tower Chambers, Westminster, has recently been founded by a few well-known art-workers, and at their rooms may be seen photographs as well as specimens of work specially relating to church decoration.

Fuller information can be obtained in "The Year's Art."

PRINTED BY J. S. VIRTUE AND CO., LIMITED, CITY ROAD, LONDON.